MAKE WITH THE BRAINS, PIERRE

Dana Wilson

Introduction by Randal S. Brandt

Black Gat Books • Eureka California

MAKE WITH THE BRAINS, PIERRE

Published by Black Gat Books
A division of Stark House Press
1315 H Street
Eureka, CA 95501, USA
griffinskye3@sbcglobal.net
www.starkhousepress.com

MAKE WITH THE BRAINS, PIERRE
Originally published by Julius Messner, Inc., New York, 1946.

ISBN: 979-8-88601-149-4

Text design by Mark Shepard, shepgraphics.com
Cover design by Jeff Vorzimmer, ¡caliente!design, Austin, Texas
Proofreading by Bill Kelly

First Stark House Press/Black Gat Edition: June 2025

"… a grim tale of psychological suspense,
reminiscent of the work of Cornell Woolrich…
a surprising accomplishment in its evocation of
the Gallic character, the postwar Hollywood lifestyle, and the elements of human tragedy."
—Bill Pronzini, *1001 Midnights*

"The story fascinated me from
beginning to end."   —Roland Young

"I found it interesting and unusual."
—Ben Hecht

"I read with the greatest enjoyment. I am a
'mystery' addict and I did not know it was
possible in this crowded field of literature to
find anything so fresh and novel as this."
—Sir Cedric Hardwicke

"I could not put it down. I had to know
what that thing in the bathtub was!"
—Dorothy Kilgallen

"Pierre narrates the story in a voice that's
convincingly European. Much of the book's
appeal lies in his commentary on American life,
especially as it manifests itself in Hollywood.
He juxtaposes cynicism and wonderment as he
tries to make sense of an alien world and its
peculiar inhabitants."
—*Reading California Fiction*

THE ORIGINAL BOND GIRL

By Randal S. Brandt

Dana Wilson's career as a mystery novelist was criminally brief. When *Make with the Brains, Pierre* was published by Julian Messner, Inc. in October 1946 it marked both the author's debut and swan song in the crime fiction field. The novel was modestly successful. Following the first edition hardcover, two cheap paperback editions appeared in 1948 and 1949 under the title *Uneasy Virtue*. Then, also in 1949, the British hardcover came out, this time re-titled as *Scenario for Murder*. While the first edition provided scant information about the writer (the only clue to Dana Wilson's identity is the author's dedication, "For Stella, Michael, and Lewis"), the British edition included a dust jacket author photograph of an attractive young woman and a biographical sketch identifying her as a "wife, mother, actress and producer" living "in Hollywood with her actor-producer husband and small son."

The novel is narrated by Pierre Bernet, a French "film cutter" who emigrated to Hollywood to escape the Nazi occupation of France and has been unable to secure work for several years. Finding himself in the middle of a love triangle—he is desperately in love with Eleanor Marr, an aspiring young actress, but Eleanor is in love with Joe Sherman, who also loves Eleanor but is already married and refuses to seek a divorce—Pierre gets involved in a blackmail plot that leads to murder. As the story begins, Pierre is in his apartment, "preparing to die," knowing that there are two men outside waiting to kill him. He is resigned to his fate, but before he leaves the safety of his room, he wants to hear from Eleanor first.

In 1986, Bill Pronzini reviewed the book in *1001 Midnights: The Aficionado's Guide to Mystery and Detective Fiction* and opined that, "despite having one of crime fiction's worst and most misleading titles," it is "neither a bad nor a whimsical nor a detective novel" but rather "a grim tale of psychological suspense reminiscent of the work of Cornell Woolrich in its incisive examination of a man destroyed by love, hate, and the dark side of his own soul." He concluded by declaring it "a surprising accomplishment in its evocation of the Gallic character, the postwar Hollywood lifestyle, and the elements of human tragedy."

The reason why Dana abandoned crime fiction is unknown. She may simply have had too many other things occupying her attention. In the years following publication of her fiction debut, she experienced the end of her first marriage, became a single mother, tried her hand at movie acting and screenwriting, and, after meeting and marrying her second husband, Albert R. Broccoli, became the guiding female voice for one of the most iconic franchises in film history.

Dana was born on January 3, 1922 as Dorothy Natoli into an Italian-Irish family in Brooklyn, New York, the second child of Giuseppe (Joseph) Natoli and Stella Natoli (née White). Shortly after her birth, the family name was shortened to Natol. Her father, known to family and friends as "Nat," was the son of Italian immigrants and a veteran of World War I. In the 1950s he had a restaurant in Los Angeles, the Forum Grill, where Dana and her mother worked as cashiers and kept the books.

Dana decided at an early age that she wanted to be an actress. After she graduated from high school, she enrolled in Cecil Clovelly's Academy of Dramatic Arts at Carnegie Hall in New York City. She soon met a fellow acting student, Lewis Gilbert Wilson, who was also studying at Carnegie Hall. They fell in love and were married on June 7, 1941 in Manhattan. As newlyweds, they moved to Maine to join Carl Friedan's company at the Rangeley Playhouse. Their son, Michael, was born the following year. After some time playing the leading roles in various New England stock companies, they decided to try their luck in Los Angeles.

Lewis was first to achieve some level of success in Hollywood. After a couple of bit parts in movies, he got his big break. In 1943, Columbia Pictures created the first live-action depiction of the DC Comics superhero Batman and Lewis was cast in the titular role in a 15-part serial, giving him the distinction of being the first actor to portray the Caped Crusader. His acting career was put on hold, however, when he was drafted into the army. He officially enlisted on June 27, 1944 at Fort MacArthur in San Pedro and was sent to Europe, where he saw action during the Battle of the Bulge. He was invalided out due to severe frostbite and spent several months in hospitals in France and England before returning home in late 1945.

Meanwhile, Dana, who was more interested in writing than in acting in movies, made the acquaintance of the Siodmak brothers, Robert and

Curt, and they both became her mentors.

Robert Siodmak was born in 1900 in Dresden, Germany; his brother Kurt (he would later change the spelling of his first name to Curt) was born in 1902. Their parents came from Jewish families in Leipzig. The brothers were both drawn to filmmaking—Robert as a director and Curt as a screenwriter—and started their careers in Germany. They fled the country in 1933. Robert established himself with the émigré cinema community in Paris; Curt relocated to London in order to work with Alfred Hitchcock. In 1937, Curt left England to become a screenwriter in Hollywood, and the brothers were reunited there in 1940. Robert Siodmak directed some of the seminal films noirs of the 1940s, such as *Phantom Lady* (1944), *The Killers* (1946—for which he was nominated for an Academy Award for Best Director), and *Criss Cross* (1949). Curt Siodmak made his name in Hollywood when he wrote the screenplay for *The Wolf Man* (1941). His 1942 novel, *Donovan's Brain*, was adapted for the screen three times.

It is unclear when, exactly, Dana met the Siodmaks, but it was likely around the time that Lewis was playing Batman. As a fellow writer, Curt, in particular, took Dana under his wing. Curt advised her on her writing and, in turn, Dana performed dialogue polishes for both brothers, as English was not their native language. When Dana decided to write her own novel, Curt mentored her and very likely influenced the development of her émigré protagonist, the French film editor Pierre. In Burt Lancaster's first scene in Robert Siodmak's *The Killers*, his character, Swede, is in his room, waiting for a pair of hitmen to come for him, resigned to his fate—an existential resignation that originated in Ernest Hemingway's short story, upon which the film is based—which strongly parallels Pierre's first scene in the novel. Given Dana's connection to the Siodmaks, the fatalistic connection between Pierre and Swede seems somewhat more than coincidental.

The Wilsons' marriage suffered from the separation during Lewis' war service, his medical recuperation, and readjustment to civilian life. In 1947, Dana, with Michael and her mother Stella, moved into a G.I. house in Pomona with Lewis, and they both joined the company of the Pasadena Playhouse. In 1948, they moved back to their home in Hollywood, which they had rented out during the war, but they split up later that year. Although the exact date of their divorce is unknown, Dana and Lewis continued to occasionally work together until Lewis remarried in 1956.

Dana's Hollywood acting career started with a bit part in a 1950 film noir called *Once a Thief*, directed by W. Lee Wilder and starring Cesar Romero, June Havoc, and Lon Chaney, Jr. Then, she got her first (and only) lead role in *Wild Women*—alternatively known under the titles *Bowanga, Bowanga* and *White Sirens of Africa*—released in 1951. She appeared opposite Lewis, who had the leading actor role. In this extremely low-budget (and truly awful) film, Lewis stars as Trent, a big game hunter on safari in Africa searching for a tribe of white amazons that he had first encountered as a boy living in the area. Dana plays the Queen, the leader of the female warriors, who gets to prance around in a tiger-print bikini and recite such regrettable lines of dialogue as "Me, Queen. Me talk white-man talk." Times must have been tough for the Wilsons for them to be involved in this film, and it must have been particularly galling for a talented writer who had previously worked crafting dialogue for Robert Siodmak.

In 1951, Dana and Lewis were both cast in a made-for-TV movie, *Trigger Tales*, which was developed as the pilot of a Western series that was not picked up. Dana had the supporting female role, in which she turned out to be the villain. Then, Lewis was cast as a regular in the TV crime series *Craig Kennedy, Criminologist*. The series was short-lived, however, airing for a single season of twenty-six 30-minute episodes. Dana guest-starred in one of the episodes near the end of the run.

After her divorce from Lewis Wilson, Dana turned much of her attention to real estate investments. She sold the Hollywood house, which she had gotten in the settlement, and ultimately owned three homes in Beverly Hills, living in one and renting out the other two. In the meantime, she was making connections with the "intelligentsia" of Los Angeles. Curt Siodmak and the Russian-American composer, Vernon Duke (Vladimir Dukelsky), were frequent visitors, and she hosted events at her home to help launch *Wisdom* magazine ("the magazine of knowledge for all America") in 1956.

Dana and Albert R. "Cubby" Broccoli met by chance in 1958, at a New Year's Eve party at the Flamingo Hotel in Las Vegas. Cubby was then a widower, his wife Nedra having succumbed to cancer two years earlier, and a single father of two young children. In Cubby's eyes, Dana was "an exquisite beauty with thick, raven hair falling around a lovely face with a pale, delicate, camellia-like skin," and he had a vague feeling that he had met her somewhere before.

Dana and Cubby had indeed met before—more than a decade earlier. In December 1947, struggling to make a living in the movie business, Cubby decided to pick up some extra cash by trying his hand at selling Christmas trees on a street corner in Beverly Hills. In his autobiography, *When the Snow Melts*, Cubby described the "incredible, memorable coincidence" that occurred during his brief stint as a tree salesman:

Early one evening, just before Christmas, a stunning-looking lady stopped at my lot to buy a tree. She had her small son with her ... Having chosen a tree, she wondered where she could get a stand for it. I offered to make one for her, nailing a couple of crossed boards together and then pinning the tree to it. We wished each other 'Happy Christmas' and she walked away into the night. No reason for me to believe I'd ever see her again. To chic beauties of that class, when you've seen one Christmas tree salesman you've seen them all. But not in this particular scenario.

For that lady, my lovely Dana, and I were destined to meet again twelve years later. She remembers my selling her that tree on the corner of Wilshire and Doheny. I recall it even more vividly. There are some customers you just cannot forget.

For Cubby, it was love at second sight. He got Dana's phone number before the night was out, but they did not meet again until a few months later, again by chance and this time at the 21 Club in New York City, where they were both with other dates. But, they planned to get together back in Los Angeles and after a whirlwind five-week courtship, they were married on June 21, 1959 in Las Vegas.

Cary Grant was the best man, and Dana's 17-year-old son Michael, who had spent the night before the wedding on the town with Cubby, was a hungover member of the wedding party. With both her son and fiancé suffering the effects of the stag night, Dana had a chance at a very different future when Cary Grant came to tell her about the situation. "I did a film once" he said, "where the best man ran off with the bride. How about it?" Dana laughed off the proposition. "As tempting as it may sound, I don't think it's going to happen this time."

That Las Vegas ceremony was the start of a stunning second act for Dana Wilson. "I married Cubby," she recalled, "and my life changed completely. I left my home in California. I left my country. I left my friends. I left everything that was familiar to me ... But I followed Cubby [to London] and I trusted him, and I knew he was going to make everything all right."

Dana immediately threw herself into her new role. She had always hoped to have a large family and insisted on formally adopting Cubby's two children, Tony and Tina. In 1960, Dana gave birth to a daughter, Barbara Dana Broccoli, and, as Cubby wrote, "now [the] family was complete."

It was at about this time that Cubby met Harry Saltzman. Cubby had long wanted to film Ian Fleming's James Bond novels, but had never been able to secure the option. Saltzman held the option, which was about to expire, but could not convince anyone to finance him. Cubby had the connections in Hollywood to get the project off the ground and the pair entered into a partnership and formed EON Productions. They also created a holding company to control the licensing and rights to the Bond films that they named Danjaq, which is a combination of their wives' first names (**Dan**a Broccoli and **Jac**queline Saltzman). They inked a deal with United Artists for $1 million on June 21, 1961—on Cubby and Dana's second wedding anniversary—and the rest is movie history.

Although Dana's name never appears in the credits of any Bond film, she was an active behind-the-scenes partner to her husband and her fingerprints are all over the series, starting from the very beginning. When Cubby and Harry were casting the lead role in the first film, *Dr. No*, they became interested in a young Scotsman with limited screen credits named Sean Connery. There are many versions of how Connery came to the producers' attention, but it is generally accepted that the key to him getting the part lay with Dana Broccoli. Cubby thought he had terrific potential, but was unsure that he had the requisite sex appeal to play James Bond. So, he asked Dana to take a look at the only footage he had available of Connery, the 1959 Disney film *Darby O'Gill and the Little People*. "Dana's reaction," Cubby recalled, "was immediate: 'That's our Bond!'" Dana confirmed this story: "I was just knocked out by [Connery]. I thought he was just incredible."

Cubby also credited Dana's experience as a writer with making contributions that were "invaluable from the start" to the creation of the cinematic Bond character. "Her input wasn't always visible," he wrote, "but the writers appreciated the help she gave them." As the series progressed, Dana continued to influence the development of scripts, making practical, informed, and helpful suggestions. As they struggled to put together a screenplay for *The Spy Who Loved Me* (fourteen writers had tried and failed to come up with a coherent story), Cubby and Dana spent hours talking and brainstorming ideas, with Dana scribbling them down on paper, and they eventually rewrote the whole story. When they presented the new script to director Lewis Gilbert, he said it was the first time a producer had come to him with a storyline that worked.

Dana often functioned as an unofficial casting director. In *For Your Eyes Only*, she recommended Topol for his role and gave final approval on casting Julian Glover. She was a big fan of Timothy Dalton and pressed Cubby to cast him as Roger Moore's successor; she also helped convince Dalton, a Shakespearean-trained actor who had doubts about what playing James Bond might do to his career, to accept the role. Many of the actresses in the series remember that she was part of the casting process and had some influence in how the women were portrayed.

She provided unswerving support and expert advice to Cubby during his legal battles with Harry Saltzman. The breakup of the Broccoli-Saltzman partnership in 1973 was marked by accusations, lawsuits, and hard feelings, and could very well have spelled the end of the franchise. Cubby credited Dana, however, with giving him the strength to see it through: "But for Dana's fantastic resources and devotion, I might have thrown in the towel. As it was, we took on the battle of a lifetime—and won."

At the 1982 Oscars ceremony, the Academy bestowed its highest honor, the Irving G. Thalberg Award, on Cubby Broccoli. Roger Moore, who was in the middle of his long run portraying James Bond, was tasked with making the presentation. In his memoir, *My Word is My Bond*, Moore remembered that Cubby and Dana "were terrified that I would make light of the situation and say something silly." Consequently, during rehearsals, "Dana sat right at the front of the auditorium to ensure I stuck to the script. I did indeed stick to the script, and Cubby accepted his award with great pride and modesty."

Following Cubby's death in 1996, Dana assumed the leadership of Danjaq and oversaw the transition of film production duties to her children, Michael G. Wilson and Barbara Broccoli, who steered the James Bond franchise until forming a new joint venture with Amazon MGM Studios in 2025.

In the 1970s, Dana returned to fiction writing, penning *Florinda*, a historical romance set in eighth-century Spain published in 1977. The novel was inspired by the legend of the Visigoth King Rodrigo and the young, beautiful Florinda, which Dana uncovered while scouting locations with Cubby for Bond, most likely in Spain for *On Her Majesty's Secret Service*. Reviews were mixed, but one critic called it "a delightful novel that is hard to put down" and speculated that playing the role of Florinda would be "any ingenue's dream." The book was never turned into a movie, but Dana, herself, adapted it into a musical that had a modestly successful run in Los Angeles in 1995 and was revived as *La Cava*, which played in the West End in 2000-2001.

On February 29, 2004, at the age of 82, Dana succumbed to cancer and died at her home in Beverly Hills, having shepherded the production of the first twenty Bond films. In a career that took her from a struggling actress to an anonymous script polisher to the author of psychological suspense fiction, Dana carved out a niche for herself in Hollywood, and made her way as a single mother. Then, in a stunning second act, she teamed up with Cubby Broccoli and became the matriarch of the most famous and successful film series in history. Not only did Dana Natol Wilson Broccoli live twice, she was the original Bond girl.

Berkeley, California
March 2025

....

Randal S. Brandt is a librarian at The Bancroft Library, the primary special collections library at the University of California, Berkeley. He catalogs rare books and has been dubbed "UC Berkeley's Crime Librarian" for his role as curator of the California Detective Fiction Collection. He has contributed introductions and author profiles to new editions of forgotten mysteries issued by American Mystery Classics (Penzler Publishers), Library of Congress Crime Classics, and Bruin Books. He was born on the exact day that Ian Fleming died.

Sources

Alpi, Deborah Lazaroff. 1998. *Robert Siodmak: A Biography, with Critical Analyses of His Films Noirs and a Filmography of All His Works.* Jefferson, North Carolina: McFarland & Company, Inc.

Brandt, Randal S. 2024. "The Mystery of Dana Wilson." *The Rap Sheet* (blog), July 2. https://therapsheet.blogspot.com/2024/07/the-mystery-of-dana-wilson.html

Broccoli, Albert R., with Donald Zec. 1998. *When the Snow Melts: The Autobiography of Cubby Broccoli.* London: Boxtree.

Cork, John, dir. 2000. "Cubby Broccoli: The Man Behind Bond." *Diamonds Are Forever,* Blu-ray Disc. Directed by Guy Hamilton. Beverly Hills, CA: Metro-Goldwyn-Mayer Studios, Inc., 2012.

d'Abo, Maryam, and John Cork. 2003. *Bond Girls Are Forever: The Women of James Bond.* New York: Harry N. Abrams, Inc.

"Dana Broccoli," Wikimedia Foundation, last modified January 8, 2025, 06:22. https://en.wikipedia.org/wiki/Dana_Broccoli

Field, Matthew, and Ajay Chowdhury. 2015. *Some Kind of Hero, 007: The Remarkable Story of the James Bond Films.* Gloucestershire: The History Press.

Duncan, Paul, ed. 2023. *The James Bond Archives*. Köln: Taschen.

Moore, Roger, with Gareth Owen. 2008. *My Word is My Bond: A Memoir.* New York: Collins.

Pronzini, Bill, and Marcia Muller. 1986. *1001 Midnights: The Aficionado's Guide to Mystery and Detective Fiction.* New York: Arbor House.

Sellers, Robert. 2019. *When Harry Met Cubby: The Story of the James Bond Producers.* Gloucestershire: The History Press.

Swanbrow, Diane J. 1978. Review of *Florinda*, by Dana Broccoli. *West Coast Review of Books* 4, no. 4 (July): 38.

Wilson, Michael G., personal communication with the author, January 27, 2025.

MAKE WITH THE BRAINS, PIERRE

Dana Wilson

1

The long shadows of the sinking sun fall over the stop signal at the crossing. And there—motionless, half-hidden behind the hibiscus tree—the man still waits. He has one hand in his pocket. His car is standing across the street. The same driver, with the small mustache, sits at the wheel reading a paper.

I walk back to my writing desk, sit down, and wonder if they have patience enough to wait for me. These few pages have to be finished before I can walk downstairs.

Everything that is going to happen is clearly pictured in my mind. He will shoot from behind the hibiscus tree. He will jump into the car. The man with the mustache will drop the paper and drive off. I will fall straight onto my face, and everything will be over quickly. While I'm falling, I'll lose consciousness. It won't hurt at all.

It makes me feel important to have two men posted there for three nights now, waiting for me to leave the house. They know I'm home. The phone rings at least twice every day. And when I pick it up, hoping it's Eleanor, I hear the click of the receiver.

I've never lived so intensely as during the two days I've waited here in my room, preparing to die. It seems to me as if life has just started.

My apartment has a living room, bathroom and kitchenette. The bed is behind the door. An iron fire escape outside the window gives the room the air of a prison cell. It's more than just a prison. It's the death house. I have to use the toilet in the hall—it has no bath.

I'd like to take a bath, but I can't go into my bathroom. The "thing" is there, and I cannot face it again. It's been there for three nights. It's lying in the tub. I left the water on a little and it runs out through the overflow, but it makes no noise at all. I can't hear it even when I try. I couldn't stand any sound from the bathroom.

Eleanor will call. That's what I'm waiting for. Something else may happen. I don't know, and I don't care. Nothing else is important anymore but Eleanor's call.

From time to time I step to the window and look down at those fools who don't know what a favor they'll be doing me.

When I arrived in California, I didn't know anything about anything. I tried to tackle it like a European country. But the difference between nations is deeper and wider than oceans. All people have noses and eyes. They walk along on two legs. But their minds work differently. I know it; I've learned it.

The country in which we are born leaves its stamp on our brain. And when we arrive somewhere else, we are already marked. What can we do about it? It is too late for us to change the brand.

Tonight, I'll take my hat and coat and walk downstairs. There's no other solution. I'll leave the "thing" in the bathroom. The man behind the tree will shoot and drive off, and I'll be relieved of a burden too big and too tiresome to carry.

I can scarcely wait. But I must hear from Eleanor first.

2

Send an American to Europe. In a couple of years you'll get back a man who is European in heart and mind. Send him to the South of France and show him how to drink *Amer Cassis*. In a few weeks you're sure to find him at lunch time, pronto, sitting in a *bistro* drinking his *apéritif*. And, mind you, slowly. A *bistro* is no drugstore! If he gets a job in London, he'll laugh about the strange English habit of drinking tea at four. But after half a year just look at him watching the clock eagerly and hear him complain when the hot water with the little brown leaves is late.

But a European in America—he'll always be a European. I've been here in California for almost three years. My knowledge of the language is not so hot. If I knew only one hundred and twenty words, I could find work as a song writer. But since I'm blessed with about a thousand, the language seems to be very difficult. Well, I can express myself fairly clearly, I hope. Most people, like Eleanor or Emily or Jerry, are kind enough, from time to time, to utter some friendly words of astonishment at how wonderfully I've mastered the language in only forty months. But I know that I'll never learn it properly; that I'll never change. My mind is anchored somewhere seven thousand miles across the sea, in a country that does not exist anymore. My way of thinking is not as direct as that of the charming people the *Saturday Evening Post* describes.

He who has two countries, has none—and I have no country. When my body was shipped to another continent, my soul got lost somewhere. It may be swimming in the sea, or perhaps it drowned. Anyhow, this man who speaks, walks, eats (not often), and works (even more rarely), and loves, is nothing more than a hollow figure shaped like a human being.

People are kind to me. If I go downstairs into the small, cheap lobby of the apartment house where I have been living for almost a year, the pretty girls and good-looking boys greet me. Some smile. Some make no sign of recognition. But I have the feeling that they all would like to speak. They're only shy and a little embarrassed about talking to a foreigner.

Among them is a very charming young girl. She is about twenty years old, a film extra. When she wears no make-up, her face is not so pretty. Her mouth has a very strange expression, as though she were disgusted with life and men. Her eyes are very dark and beautiful, her legs too heavy, but her body above the hips is frail and like that of a seventeen-year-old. When she returns from work, tired, with the heavy studio make-up still on her face—too worn out to clean up before dinner—her beauty is radiant, the bone structure of her face more than beautiful.

Her name is Emily. But at thirty-four I'm much too old for her. My hair is thinning and my temples are a little gray. Young girls don't like signs of age. All they have is their youth, and not to be twenty or twenty-three anymore is an unforgivable crime. Youth is success, youth is something to be proud of. But what do they do with their youth? I don't know. They are young as though being young were their profession.

When I went to the beach with Eleanor one day, she glanced at my body and said with subtle surprise: "You don't look bad for your age!" That was something to conjure with. I can't forget it. For the first time I felt old.

We had a hamburger at a drive-in. How I hate that stuff! They put lettuce leaves on the ground meat to hide its cheapness. The lettuce gets warm and tastes like wet tissue paper. But it fills your stomach and keeps reminding you for hours that you've had dinner.

My little jalopy is a Ford two-seater, vintage: nineteen hundred and thirty-one. But it enables me to invite Eleanor for a hamburger in a drive-in. If I had a Buick or even a Dodge, she'd ask for something better, because she hates hamburgers too. This is one of the few things we have in common, but somehow she likes me. All the young girls have a "yen" for me because I am not quite like the other boys they know. They are curious and would like to go out with me. They ask difficult questions they would never think of asking Jerry or Manny if they drove to the beach with them. They believe me highly intelligent, packed with the wisdom of an old culture.

"Gosh!" said Eleanor. "Damn, I forgot to phone Central Casting. Have you got a private phone in your room?"

I drove her home very fast, because you never know why they want to come to your room. In France, in England, especially in Italy, I'd be sure. But here in Los Angeles, she might really want to telephone. And it was so! She couldn't get there quickly enough. She wouldn't even wait for the elevator. As soon as I had unlocked my door, Eleanor rushed in, grabbed the phone and began to dial.

I sat down and watched her. How beautiful these girls are! The perfect profile, slender hips, long legs, beautiful hands, eyes of the deepest color, with a hidden fire, small and firm breasts whose outline they love to show. Their beauty is their merchandise. From hick towns and cities they come to Hollywood to sell their beauty before the camera, and here they are, getting thirty dollars a week if they are lucky.

Eleanor kept on dialing the number, again and again, until the movement of her hand blurred before my eyes.

"You have to keep on trying," she said, looking up from under the bandanna which, askew, covered her blond hair. "Eleanor Marr," she said quickly, listened for a moment and hung up. I didn't notice at first, but when I looked more closely I found her crying. Her face was wet with tears.

"It's your fault," she said. "You with your rotten beach and your vile hamburgers! They've already called another girl . . ." She was desperate.

She told me that when a studio called for her, the call was kept for half an hour. If she didn't call back in that time, the call was given to someone else. That's what had happened; ten and a half dollars gone down the drain! And she needed the money badly.

"I'll give you ten bucks," I consoled her.

Her eyes began to light up. "I can't take it from you," she said, but her eyes contradicted her. "You have no money yourself!"

I opened my checkbook and wrote a check to cash. She looked wonderingly at the yellow paper.

"You're a fool," she said dryly and snatched it out of my hand. "I'll take it just to teach you! And you won't get anything for it. Even if I liked you, I couldn't!"

"I understand!" I looked at her, amused.

"You *don't* understand. You foreigners are all wolves. You think when a girl comes up to your room you understand exactly why."

I looked at her silently. I could not follow her thoughts. Something was wrong, something worried her, and it broke out in this strange way.

"Let's go"—I smiled at her comfortingly—"if you don't feel like staying. I'll take you wherever you want to go! Don't think I'm a roué . . . I'm only half as bad as my reputation!"

She took off her bandanna. Her face clouded with unhappiness. She walked toward the window and sat down on the divan, looking at me inquisitively.

"There's something I like about you and something I can't stand," she said. "I wish I could love you, just so I could find out what it is."

"Why don't you? I wouldn't be anything but an experiment for you," I laughed. "I promise I'll do my very best!"

"Skip it!" she said, but kept on watching me. "Why did you give me that check? To show off?"

"That's it," I nodded. "I get a big kick out of it, showing off with ten dollars."

"But you have no money—I know." She said it as though she had discovered the ultimate wisdom of the world.

"I got my last pay check six months ago."

"And this money?"

"It's a major part of my immense fortune!" I knew it was no disgrace among poor people to be poor.

She continued cross-examining me. "Why did you give me the money? Did you hope I'd sleep with you?"

"When there's no more hope, there's no more life!" I laughed. She was so serious, and so keen to analyze my intentions. She could not imagine that the impulse of a moment often makes me do things which afterwards looked carefully planned. She was a kid, grown up among people who didn't give something for nothing. She couldn't understand such a thing. She tortured her little brain to classify me among the friends she had known. Obviously I didn't fit.

She waited a minute, and because I didn't move and didn't try to kiss her, she sighed a little and tore the check slowly to pieces. I looked at her mouth, her generous lips, her strong white teeth, and for a moment I considered grabbing her, kissing her. Her eyes took on a peculiar soft, wet look and seemed to become darker. She lay down on the divan, folded her legs under her; her skirt did not cover her knees.

"You're such a helpless fool I'll have to do something for you," she decided, and for a moment I understood her. She was unapproachable, here in my room where the waning light of the day cast long shadows on her face, making her still more beautiful.

"You'd better go," I said, and something in my voice made her feel that she had me where she wanted every man to be.

"Why . . ." She turned her face toward me. "You can kiss me once because I like you!" I kissed her but she held her teeth closed and pushed me back. "Not like that!" she said. "Sit there in the chair, silly, and behave! Let's see what we can do for you."

I looked into her blue eyes. She had won and was content. I felt a burning desire to slap her. She was like a frozen fish, and she had to find another fish to get excited.

"What did you do before?" she asked.

The room was getting darker. Her white face swam in the dying light, changed shape and proportions.

"I come from France, you know," I said.

She smiled softly and put her hand on mine; curiously enough, she seemed to realize that it was hurting me to talk about it.

"Well, three years ago some big shots from Hollywood came to Paris—guys who were so important that they had lost all sense of proportion. I met them. We went out together, and they had a great time. It was just an evening like any other to me, but for them it was 'gay Paree.' They loosen up when they're abroad and forget their respectability. They bought everything they could lay their hands on—women and men and jewels and clothes and antiques. They didn't care what they bought because to them everything was a bargain. That's why they went mad buying . . . and they bought me, too."

"Why?" she asked. Her question showed me my futility.

"Very nicely put," I said. "The truth is, your question is justified. One got me for a year, and what he didn't pay he made up for with promises. He wanted me to build up his Foreign Department. I was foolish enough to fall for it. You know—Hollywood is like Seventh Heaven; it's magic. We in Europe fall for it just like you little girls from Middletown.

"Well, I arrived and waited around for six months. Then I found out they didn't need a Foreign Department. I got desperate and they let me cut films, and promoted me to Foreign Adviser. 'Can Louis the Fifteenth kick Marie Antoinette in the slats'? they asked me. When I said no, they did it anyhow because it's such a nice scene. They'll do anything for a nice scene. They even let people go to hell for a good gag.

"Then war broke out. France died.... I lost my job and got a bagful of promises. And here I am, slowly getting hysterical. Everybody in this town gets hysterical because they think they'd starve if they left here. That's why they cut each other's throats all the time. They're hounded with fear . . . a fear that kills friendship and decency. They lose all sense of proportion. This town has only two dimensions, like a motion picture. It's not human—it's a freak! It's—"

I controlled myself, seeing her blue eyes widen, watching me, catching me off guard.

"Successful people don't talk like this"—I tried to laugh it off—"only people with their backs against the wall...."

"You're no fool," she said, and withdrew her hand. I could feel her putting her brains to work; even in the dark I could see that she was trying hard to think. "Did you save any money?" Clear and practical, she thought first of the essentials.

"Well—what do you expect after six months without a job?"

"And if you can't find a job?"

"It's easy to get an invitation for lunch, more difficult to get one for dinner, and impossible to get breakfast. For a nice girl like you it's a cinch to get dinner and breakfast. Lunch is a little more difficult."

"Can't you be serious for a minute?" She did not like my humor. "I'll ask Joe to give you a job. I bet he'll do something if I ask him."

"Who is Joe?" I didn't take her promise seriously. I only wanted to make her talk. I liked the whiteness of her teeth shining in the dark.

"Joe is the man I love," she said dreamily. There was silence. I hated her. I felt myself superfluous. I had the same feeling once in Paris when I was sitting in a taxicab with two girls, and the girls, bending forward, kissed each other, disregarding me completely. I felt rotten and could do nothing but laugh at myself.

"Why are you laughing?" she asked sharply, sitting up.

"Because it's a silly situation. If you could only look at yourself with my eyes—at the line of your shoulder, at your mouth, your hair. Alone in a dark room with a beautiful girl, and sitting in a chair three yards away from her! It's so ridiculous I have to laugh. I beg your pardon. It's strictly against the laws of nature!"

She slid back on the couch, perfectly happy.

"You like me," she said.

I moved toward her and kissed her. Her face was soft. All I wanted was to kiss her gently. I felt so desperately lonely, and the kiss assured me that I was not entirely lost.

"Be sensible," she said soberly, and pushed me away with both hands. "Think of me for a moment, please."

I could not see her face. It was completely dark now. I only felt her soft hair in my hands, her body in my arms.

"I wish somebody were here who loved me, really loved me . . ." she said with a sigh. She couldn't have hit me harder with a hammer, and I let go of her at once.

"What about Joe? Shall I ring him up?"

She slipped her hand gently into mine, and that little gesture of intimacy softened all the ill feeling I had.

"No—that's impossible—you see—Joe is married, but he loves me more than anything in the world."

"If he loves you so much, why is he still married?" I asked, trying to hurt her.

"Because his religion forbids adultery," she said

seriously.

"Most religions do," I said, amused, "but still . . ."

"He belongs to a religious sect whose members would rather die than be unfaithful. His wife wanted a divorce before he met me. He is very kind, he really is. I have talked to him so much, and sometimes he seems even more intelligent than you. He never touches me. You're the first man I've kissed in a year. I shouldn't do it! Joe told me, 'Whatever you do in your life, think of me. I'll always be at your side, reminding you'!"

"What a horrible thing to say!" I was shaken. I felt that this man exercised a power over the girl which was sadistic.

"I haven't seen him for a long time. He phones me every day and asks if he can do anything for me. He'll get his divorce soon. You believe that, don't you?" she said, wanting to be reassured.

"Of course," I said.

All she had in her life was the hope that Joe, a religious fanatic, would marry her someday. But at least she had something to live for, which was more than I had.

"Joe had asked so often how he can help me. Tomorrow when he calls, I'll ask him to do something for you. He'll do it, I'm sure."

For a foreign film cutter to get a job, a fanatic had to fall in love with an extra girl!

"If he gets me work, you shall have your commission—dinner at the Beachcomber's. Think of it! A real Hawaiian dinner!"

I lifted her up and switched on the lights. She didn't look as beautiful as she had before. Her eyes were red from crying. She went into the bathroom and brushed her hair. I followed her, looking over her shoulder into the mirror. I put my arm around her, but she went on brushing, watching herself.

"What a face!" she said. "I couldn't look any worse if I'd stayed here all night. Look at the wrinkles under my eyes!"

She turned around and kissed me innocently. "Good night, Pierre!"

"Good night, Eleanor!"

"I think I'll have to find a girl for you." She smiled kindly.

"That's not a bad idea. I live like a monk.... Funny town, Hollywood . . . too many girls around—seven and a hunchback for every man. And even so you find only sex-starved men."

"You're not in circulation, that's all." She laughed. "Do you like Emily?"

There was something like fear in her eyes. My God, she couldn't expect to have everything!

"Emily is sweet—but too young for me."

"Don't be silly. She likes you. She talks about you a lot."

"She didn't give me that impression—but perhaps I'm not observant enough." I thought of Emily's dark, sad eyes. But Eleanor should know better. What did I really know about these girls? They are, obviously, a secret club which no man can ever penetrate.

"Let's knock at her door. She's home."

I tried to be as casual as possible. "All right," I said.

Before we left the room, Eleanor held me back.

"You're a bastard," she said, "going from one girl to the other. Maybe that's better—why should you be faithful to me? I certainly haven't given you any reason. Besides, I'd rather have you with a girl I know than with one I don't."

She tried to smile at me, still hesitating, lifting her face soberly. I felt like a heel. I could have kicked myself. What the hell was the matter with me lately? I had lost my nerve. This hopeless sitting around and waiting for something to happen was making me crack up.

When I lost my job, my agent said, "I'll get you something. You'll soon be working again. All you have to do is wait and keep your nerve." But my nerves were swiftly going to hell. I had only one friend— Eleanor. Why did I try so hard to hurt her? She was kind to me. Kinder than I deserved.

"Sometimes I behave like a pig, hate myself for it, but feel relieved in spite of it," I said. It was no excuse. I only wanted her to know how I felt.

"Won't you come with me to see Emily?" There was so much hope and suppressed anxiety in her voice that I felt comforted and very good.

"You should know me by now," I said. And it sounded like a joke.

She still held the doorknob in her hand.

"Will you permit me?" she asked, with a smile I won't forget.

She put her arms around me and kissed me. I didn't move. She had very little technique; she was completely unspoiled. But she put her soul and her gratitude into the kiss.

Still, I didn't even put my arms around her. She withdrew, then kissed my cheeks—twice on the left, once on the right.

"Left—right—left," she laughed. "You tell me that doesn't mean a thing in France. Good night, Pierre."

"Good night, Eleanor. Be faithful to me."

"I will!"

I listened to her quick, light steps as she went down the passage.

3

The elevator came up, humming deeply. There was still time to call Eleanor back, but I waited and listened, battling the desire to run after her. Now the elevator went down again. I turned and looked around at my room. What a fool I was to play the righteous man—I could have been sitting in Emily's room now. Even to behave like a skunk was better than to be here alone with the dark, worn furniture, smoke-stained curtains, and the iron fire escape outside the window. It was a room furnished especially for people who wanted to commit suicide. Even inside a coffin I should have had a better view.

I went into the kitchen and opened the icebox. There was some bacon, hiding trichinae under yellow lard; some bread, stale and wet and cold; and a bottle of beer. I gulped down the beer, stuffed my mouth with bacon, and left the room. Jerry was home, I hoped.

He was in his room, shaving and whistling. Jerry had no job either. I don't know what he lived on, but he had the faculty of regarding life as a pleasant trip to hell and enjoying the journey thoroughly. I think he was an actor. He thought so, too. He had acted several times. I can remember him playing opposite Marjorie Dean, who is a top star now. He played the part of a man who was in bondage to his wife and who drove his car against a wall to kill himself and her because she was going to leave him for good. He succeeded so well in killing himself that he never appeared in another picture; while she, saved by the author's grace, carried on to become a great star.

Here in America, the problems are love, marriage and divorce. There's no other conflict—the question is how to get her, how to marry her, and how to get rid of her again. That fills books and magazines, films and plays. The happy stories end where tragedy actually begins: with marriage. And the dreary ones with a happy conclusion: divorce or death. Before a boy can sleep with a girl, he must marry her, or at least promise marriage. That's the law of the Hays office. If you can't live a proper life yourself, at least create a fictitious one. Couples whose combined ages are not more than thirty-five years look at these moral movies.

"Hello!" said Jerry, grinning into the mirror. "What's up, stranger? No girl tonight?"

"Have you ever seen me with a girl?" I asked, relieved to speak to someone who would not bother me with the difficult problems of an empty life, making issues out of nothing.

If I should ever want to remember some commendable quality about Jerry, this would be it. It might be the only one, but it was important to me.

"Didn't you just go up with a very cute number? Through already?"

He did not move a muscle of his face as he carefully shaved his chin.

"Nothing doing with her. She's an angel. She's in love with somebody else," I said. I did not like to make or hear any cracks about her.

Jerry turned around.

"The trouble is," he said seriously, "that you boys from over there make love to these girls. You shouldn't! Don't promise them anything. It's fatal. You'll never get rid of them—and besides, you're spoiling them for decent people like me."

"And how do you do it?"

"Well—I just tell 'em that this is nothing but animal desire. I want 'em and tell 'em so. If they refuse, that's their right; it's just too bad for them! But I'd never tell 'em I was in love with 'em, or lower myself to discuss intelligent questions, as you fellows do. They're not complicated. They're simple. They follow the same pattern. If you want to have 'em around temporarily, be aloof, indifferent, and don't phone them. That intrigues them for a while. It drives them crazy, but their vanity can't take it very long and then they get tired and drift. You never have any trouble with them that way. If you make a big play for them and then cool, brother—that's murder!"

He grinned into his mirror again. He took pleasure in being cynical.

I watched him finish shaving. He was a good-looking boy, with a smooth face and a chin like a boxing glove. For a while he had been bodyguard to a well-known actor who often got drunk and had to be kept out of rows. Jerry had to take him home at a certain time, even against his will.

"Want one?" he asked, carefully selecting a tie from a rack which bulged. Even the poorest fellow here has ties—it's no sign of wealth. They pile up like books.

I shook my head. I think he divined my loneliness, but never talked about it. In fact, we never discussed any serious question. It would have spoiled our friendship.

"What are you going to do tonight?"

"Nothing special—hang myself, maybe."

"You'll have plenty of time tomorrow for that. Come

with me tonight. I've found a sucker who pays for drinks and invites all kinds of people. I intend to get nicely drunk, like a gentleman. He'll pay, all right. He just loves to! And you're coming with me!" There was kindness in his insistence.

"I don't see much fun in that . . ." I began, afraid to go back to my room.

"You'll be surprised—he'll take us all to his house later on. There you'll see something. They say he can't sleep. He never sleeps more than a couple of hours, and he drinks all the time to prepare himself for the night. He has dough, that boy! He certainly has it. I don't like his face, but his liquor's okay."

"You win!" I said, suddenly excited. Perhaps I could get drunk. That meant more than just passing a night. I'd sleep until lunch time and spend the day in a fog. Hope for tomorrow!

"Let's go," he said; "but if he finds a girl he likes, don't butt in. He's very touchy about that!"

"I've no intention whatsoever of butting in. He can have 'em all. Who are these girls?"

"Tarts." He shook his head. To him this seemed a superfluous question.

He took me to the Jazz Club. The door has a peephole through which the bouncer could see us. He opened for us at once. They knew Jerry well.

We went inside. About a dozen girls in evening dress were sitting along the bar, looking bored. Jerry talked to a Swedish girl from Brooklyn whose name was Robin; she was a sad beauty with natural blond hair. She looked at me with the same blank expression the other girls wore. I still had two dollar bills in my pocket, and for the moment I didn't give a damn about anything. This is the state of mind I enjoy most. You just don't care, and you float along. Whatever you do, it's all right. You feel happy and loquacious, like a full-fledged member of a community of human beings. There's no tomorrow; nothing to tie your mind down to earth.

I was brilliant. I felt very superior to all these halfwits clustered around the bar. I was out to impress Robin, and she opened her heart at once. I am cursed with having to listen to the heartaches of all the people in the world. Nobody ever speaks about me; they all talk about themselves.

I could start a big business by opening a shop on Hollywood Boulevard where people could talk about themselves to me for, say, a dollar an hour. I would soon have branches all over town, all over America; would become an international institution for frustrated souls.

Concentrating on Robin without clearly hearing what she said, I already felt myself a millionaire. I was busy giving the impression of a careful listener, and this took most of my attention.

She told me about Jerry. The first evening he met her he had asked her point-blank to marry him. She didn't have a very good opinion of him: he was a bum and a moocher. But somewhere deep in a heart covered with the wreckage of a destroyed youth, she seemed to like him for that proposal. It had touched something in her that was still clean. Suddenly she changed the subject and spoke about Fred Marshall, the man the whole bar was waiting for.

Marshall was giving her money to learn to sing, and he expected her to report here every night. Why, she didn't know. He had no other designs on her, she said. Jerry also lived off Marshall; in fact, the whole bar seemed to live off him.

Robin turned her pale face toward the glass, sucked the liquor through a straw. I wondered why she was sitting here. Her beauty was classic. She was too good for such an atmosphere. But you can't help anybody who is not psychologically prepared to be helped. Her fate was to look beautiful, to waste away in a second-rate nightclub.

It was like applause when Fred Marshall arrived. A whispering went through the room, and everybody seemed to be gayer. Marshall greeted Jerry. Hilariously, Jerry introduced me, and Marshall, who was slightly drunk, gripped my hand as if I were his lost brother. He ordered drinks. A big glass standing in front of him quickly filled with bartenders' slips. All the girls joined the party. They flirted with him. He was guarded like the termite queen by all the other termites. He couldn't speak a word without being listened to attentively. He seemed to enjoy being in the limelight, but he never showed off.

I watched him. In his ugly face, his eyes were like dirty, frozen water. His expression was cruel. He seemed carefully to avoid getting sober. Drinking like a fish, he did not get drunk like an ordinary human being. His surface was hard, but he had not entirely drowned his conscience.

I caught his glance when he looked quickly at me. With the watchful eyes of a suspicious man, he took my measure, and seemed to know at once what was wrong with me. He was not asleep. By God, he was not! He was just watching us from behind a veil of drunkenness as if we were marionettes dangling from his fingers. He had Robin on his right arm, and a dark-haired girl with voluptuous lips on his left. She was sensual, in a vulgar way, and the only one who really interested me. Marshall found that out at once and concentrated on her. She played up to him, but pressed my arm behind his back.

I got drunk. After the bar had closed, we crawled into Marshall's car, and he drove down Sunset Boulevard at a terrific speed. The girls giggled and shrieked, and I expected a crash at any moment. I didn't care. I was awake again, waiting with a curious hope for the accident. What a noisy end it would be! Quick and very satisfactory! I'd have the good excuse that fate had prevented me from fulfilling my life's duties.

But such a convenient death is too good for a wretch like me. We arrived safely.

Marshall lived in a pompous house in Beverly Hills. But here, where even beggars dwell in mansions with swimming pools, this was no indication of his wealth. Lights were burning in every window. A Filipino boy opened the door. We all floated inside and made as much noise as possible.

Standing beside our host, I suddenly saw blood on his lips. He wiped it off with his handkerchief. Some sixth sense warned him that I was watching, and I looked up into eyes so packed with hatred and fury that I sobered for a moment. He threw the soiled handkerchief at his Filipino and stalked out of the room.

Square-shouldered and big-chested, he didn't look like a man with TB. His cheeks were rather round, his eyes deep-set, his lips a vivid red, his hands short-fingered and thick.

I followed him reluctantly into the living room and stopped in the doorway. The furniture was made of glass. The tables had glass tops and green bases. Even the piano was made of glass and showed its guts like a cadaver at an autopsy. Every chair had glass legs. The radio case was transparent, and I could see the tubes and wiring. For a moment I was completely bewildered. I had never seen anything like it before. It was so ugly I felt like gagging. Even the room changed its color and the crazy people in it seemed to be transparent, too. I saw the heart beating in Robin's breast, and the intestines of our host were made of glass. The illusion vanished at once. I shouldn't have had so much Pernod.

"Don't stare at Marshall, you fool. He doesn't like to be stared at," Jerry whispered at my side, and pulled me around. "He always bleeds at the mouth. A gangster friend shot him in the stomach when he was a lawyer in New York, and they replaced his guts with silver. He should have been dead a long time ago, but fortunately he isn't. I must get a hundred bucks out of him tonight, so don't stare at him and spoil my chances."

I walked over to the bar and Robin handed me a glass. Her eyes were sad and very promising. She felt that I had no designs on her, and, having nothing else herself, like any of those other beautiful girls, she flirted with me and put her soft arm around my shoulder. "*Skaal!*" she said. It was the only Swedish word she knew, I bet! But it fitted her blond hair. I gulped the drink down. It was Pernod again and I was drunk in a second.

"Will you take me home—afterwards?" she asked, and looked at me with eyes like a Lorelei. I smiled and walked away. You should always show those tarts you don't need them.

Stopping to regain my composure, I looked at a picture. I had seen that girl's face before, but I couldn't place it. It was much more alive than Robin's—high cheekbones, a full mouth with delicate, turned-up corners, made broader and more dominant with lipstick, hair deeply pointed into a round forehead, intelligent eyes that seemed to follow you wherever you went in the room.

"To Fred, with gratitude!" I read, in girlish writing across the picture. It was too ornate to be natural. I don't know anything about American graphology. Every language has its own laws about it. If this were the writing of a French girl, I'd think her conceited and preposterously artificial. But in America? She might write with her left hand, and how could I know what to read from that? A school might have taught her that bold stroke.

"Do you know her?" It was Marshall behind me. I didn't answer. I didn't even turn my head. I tried to snub him. Men like him have to be snubbed. He couldn't buy me with a drink.

"It's Marjorie Dean," he said and looked at me curiously. There was no blood on his lips now. "She's beautiful . . . isn't she?"

She was a star, too highly paid.

"So what?" I said rudely. "Look at Robin—beautiful too—and look at that other girl there. Gorgeous! Beauty is cheap in this town. I'm fed up with beauty. Their flawless, empty faces leave me cold and their long, blood-red nails turn my stomach."

Marshall looked at the picture. "Like to meet her?" He was determined to make conversation about her. Obviously he was fascinated by her. He pushed the picture flat with his left hand, covering its face. It was a very possessive gesture, and in my fogged mind I remembered Jerry's warning.

"She's getting five grand a week," I said quite nonchalantly. "She can buy nearly everything she wants. Why bother about her? She can look after herself. I don't think she'd be any fun. I know those women. I resent their masculine attitude. I don't like their independence. I take pride in my virility. I like making love, not being made love to." I pushed his hand away. "They don't think of you—only themselves. I don't like them."

Marshall still had his ugly grin, but I had made some impression on him. He seemed to like me, if it were possible for him to like anyone.

Through the door came music; strange and warbling. Three Filipino boys—his servants—were sitting in a corner, playing on flat guitars and singing. The lights went out and only a blue glow shone from the transparent table stems. Every face looked ghastly. What a treat for the girls!

Out of the heap of women and men who were piled up in the corner next to the piano, the girl with the broad lips emerged. She had taken her dress off, and her slip was nothing but a bluish veil. Very drunk and in a kind of trance, she began to dance, and did it well. I suppose she had a touch of the tarbrush. Probably that's why her face had seemed so interesting. She danced as I had never seen anyone dance before. That drop of dark blood gradually took possession of her. The Filipinos never looked up.

I felt low in spite of my drunkenness. There was still some hidden decency in me and it tortured me. I stared at the girl. Her sensual mouth became more and more prominent, the shadows emphasized her high cheekbones, her eyes grew slanter and darker, her teeth brighter, stronger. Her whole face changed, assuming the characteristics of another race. She had forgotten where she was, what she was doing. There was nothing but rhythm, nothing but moving sex. She didn't dance for us; she danced for herself. The girl was much closer to the Filipino boys than to us; she didn't belong to us anymore. There was a broad barrier which not only I, but Marshall, seemed to perceive.

The Filipinos played, bent over their instruments. One sang an unearthly tune; the others joined in. The music no longer made sense to my ears. The girl's body moved convulsively, faster and faster. It transferred its momentum to me. I felt a cramp in my chest, caught myself following the rhythm with my whole body. I despised the dancing girl, hated her because I was bound to the ground, too heavy to float.

Marshall seemed to feel the same. He suddenly called out, his voice filled with fury: "Enough!"

Lights were switched on at once. The girl came to, and smiled sheepishly. Nobody paid any more attention to her. She went into a corner and put on her dress. I felt rotten and took another drink.

Robin was standing at the bar, watching me with a weary and forlorn expression. I could easily have taken her with me, but I squeezed myself out of the room and left the house. Why had I left so suddenly? I was sober again. At home I would have to face the empty walls until I felt like suicide. Even so, it would be better than staying.

The night was fresh. The cool dampness hit me hard across the face. Being halfway between drunkenness and a clear mind, I walked toward Hollywood. Beverly Hills was silent. The big houses, hidden behind fences of palm trees, were dark. With their bare stems and feathery tops, the palms looked like Zulu warriors. They were old. It took a long time to become so naked and to carry these war insignia.

My steps echoed hollowly from across the street. I walked down Alpine Drive toward Sunset, when suddenly a car drove quietly up behind me. I felt someone looking at me. The car passed me and stopped. A policeman stepped out and waited for me. I marched along without paying any attention to him.

"Hey!" he called out as I came up to him.

I stopped. I hate the police. They're so cocksure. The whole town seems to have been created only to make them important. Their job is to bully people who cannot defend themselves. They are so small that they continually have to convince themselves that they are big by bullying people. That's an international characteristic of the police. They were once created by the citizenry, but now the citizens seem to have been created for them. Only in England do they bother to be polite. In England you're even allowed to tell a cop what you think of him.

"My name is not 'Hey.' You must be mistaken," I said. I had heard shocking stories of people being beaten up for nothing by these mongrels. But there was a new mayor in town and I dared to be bold.

"Sarcastic, huh?" he said, and played his flashlight on me. "What are you doing here, walking through Beverly Hills?"

I saw red for a moment.

"There're still people in this town who can't afford a car. Savvy? If everybody had a car, you wouldn't have a chance to annoy people who're taking a walk."

"Foreigner, huh?" he asked, and shoved the flashlight

closer to my face.

"Ask your father or your grandfather if they were foreigners, too. Or are you an Indian?" I felt so angry that I had to hold myself back to keep from lunging at him. But what was the use? He'd only have socked me.

"You're drunk!" he concluded.

"Well—I'm not driving a car, and I was careful enough not to run into you!" I replied. But I didn't feel very comfortable.

"What're you doing here? You know we've got to watch everybody who's prowling around. There's too many burglars. If anything happens, they blame us."

He appealed to my sympathy and I was sorry for him. I nearly broke into tears.

"If I were a burglar, at least I'd have a car," I said and laughed, trying to be good friends with him. "I'd certainly rather ride home than walk.... Why don't you give me a lift?"

He found that so extraordinarily funny that he had to laugh too. He was a husky fellow with a well-fed stomach that shook visibly in the dark.

"I'll give you a ride—if you don't live downtown," he said, showing his human side.

"I live on Cherokee," I said.

He went back to the car and talked to his buddy. They offered me a lift.

What a night!

4

The shrill telephone bell woke me. It cut short a nightmare, letting me forget what it was. Only the pressure of something ugly and horrible weighed on my mind. The sun shone through the thin curtains. It was sickeningly hot.

Again the phone rang.

"Mr. Bernet?" a strange voice asked, pronouncing it like Bennett. "My name is Joe . . ." The voice paused a moment. "Joe Sherman." It waited again to give me time to place the name, and the phone was quiet for some time. This is a trick many people play—to wait and force others to talk.

It was Joe—Eleanor's Joe! I suddenly saw a black wall opening, looked into a landscape of trees and springs and a clear sky, very romantic. A premonition struck me. I felt light and was suddenly happy without any obvious cause. Subconsciously, I always know about things to come, as many people do. If you train yourself to listen to the faint seismographic vibrations of your soul indicating in advance good and bad occurrences, nothing can surprise you. You're prepared, even if you don't know what you're prepared for; you're on your guard. Joe's voice prepared me for the shock of something to happen—something pleasant.

"Pierre Bernet speaking. How're you, Mr. Sherman?" In repeating his name, I told him that I knew him, and in putting life into my voice, I showed him I could do things.

"Well," the man said hesitatingly, "would you mind coming over? I may have something for you. Anyhow, let's talk about it, if you're not too busy. Please choose your own time."

If time was money, I was the richest man in the world. Rockefeller and Morgan are paupers in comparison to me. I had an *embarrass de richesse* of time!

"Whenever you say." The shock was so great that I didn't even have time to feel happy about it; my reaction was simply mechanical.

"My office is on Santa Monica Boulevard, the World Film Laboratory Corporation, you know," he said, and I didn't have the courage to tell him that I hadn't heard about this flourishing enterprise.

"I most certainly do know it. I'll be there this morning."

"That's fine," Joe said. "I'm expecting you. I know all about your work for M-G-M. See you later. Good-bye, Mr. Bernet."

This time he pronounced my name correctly. "Good-bye, Mr. Sherman," I said.

There I was, sitting stark naked, feeling a strange, burning joy. Work! It meant work, hard work, and getting tired in a beautiful way. It meant money, a new lease on life, self-assurance—everything! Eleanor had done this for me. I felt a strange pang in my chest when I whispered her name. She had done it for me! She had talked to Joe, and Joe was going to arrange something for me, to make her happy in his small and subtle way! To please her, he was rescuing me. By helping one human being, he made three happy. You should always do your best, you should always go out of your way to do kind things for other people. It makes your soul float; it makes you realize that you're not just swimming dreamily through life, but that you are a member of a community of kind people who assist each other.

So he knows all about what I have done for M-G-M. Well—he knows it! They seem to know everything about everyone here in Hollywood—what you do, how much money you're earning, with whom you sleep, where you eat, and where you get your trousers pressed. He knows my work. Miraculous!

Or—does he only want an excuse? Does he say this to prevent me from mentioning Eleanor? Is he trying to put our future business relations on the solid ground of M-G-M, and not on my knowing Eleanor? He needs an excuse to get me a job because he is married. Eleanor is no excuse, but M-G-M is. He doesn't want me to mention Eleanor. Well—that's all right with me. If he doesn't talk about her I'll gladly cut out my tongue before I'll mention her name.

I've never seen Sherman before. His name is English. Perhaps his forefathers were Puritans. I liked him already. He's determined to give me a job. Life has its pleasant sides. Sometimes the outlook is foggy. Just wait, and everything will be in order. Wait and hope. Here it is. Work!

I whistled. He who whistles in the morning will be caught by the hawk in the evening, my grandmother used to say. She hated happy people. But why not always be happy? All the months I had passed in fear of starvation—what of it? It's stupid to get frightened. It was futile torture, now that I look back. Useless! I only wore out my nerves. Why not wait patiently until everything straightens itself out? I had been foolish. I'd never be a fool again.

I took a shower and massaged my body with a brush as hard as I could. That filthy Pernod was still in my blood. After eight hours you get rid of the nicotine; after twenty, of the alcohol in your blood stream. I soon felt great. It was ten o'clock. I made myself a cup of strong coffee, and stole the paper from next door. They are nightclub dancers who always sleep until noon. I believe they're married. By the time they get up, fresh news has come out. They sleep faster than the news before their door.

Well, I sat down to eat my breakfast. Any other day I had no breakfast, hating to eat alone. Or I just had a glass of milk, not even sitting down, stuffing my mouth with anything I found in the icebox.

But today was a holiday!

A white shirt. A colored tie from Paris. The white trousers. I felt grand. A job was waiting for me! I shaved, hunting every obstinate hair down to its roots. Powder, shaving lotion. What a morning! It was really a pity to finish dressing and get on with the day. Well—there was still Jerry to visit. I hoped he was home!

Jerry's door was unlocked, as usual. He never bothered to press the little knob of the handle. Nobody would steal him anyway, he used to say, and if they should, at night, they certainly would return him with the first light when they saw what they had.

As usual, he slept with closed windows. He detested fresh air in his bedroom. Every dog puts its nose under its tail and every bird hides its bill in its feathers, and an Arab pulls his burnouse over his head—this was Jerry's excuse.

He must have been pretty drunk, because the room looked messy—clothes all over the place. But not only his clothes. There were a handbag and a blouse and a skirt lying around.

He really should have locked the door. His sense of privacy should have told him that. I tried to tiptoe out, when he suddenly looked up, staring at me. I saw blond hair pressed deep into the pillow next to him. Robin!

He pointed toward the bathroom and left the bed stealthily, so as not to wake her.

"Why don't you lock the door?" I said, passing the buck to him.

"Why should I?" He shrugged his broad shoulders. He turned on the shower. He was a very well-built boy with broad and straight shoulders, about twenty-seven years old, when the body still holds together no matter how it is misused.

"You were wise to sneak out. Marshall saw you go. It impressed him, because that crowd is only after his drinks, and nobody would ever dream of quitting before he's thrown out. At first I thought you had picked up a dame, but Robin told me you went off alone. She was disappointed; you should have had the decency to take her with you. Tonight she called me Pierre twice! After your big lecture on Freud, I'm on the lookout for these things. Calling me by other people's names! What the hell is so fascinating about you? All the girls talk about you." He looked at me with real curiosity.

"I don't know," I said, sitting comfortably on the edge of the tub. I was flattered, but tried not to show it. "They can't gossip about my qualities, because I never reveal my true self to them. And I'll keep that a secret as long as I can afford it."

"You look happy this morning," he said, lathering himself.

"I'm getting a job—today," I said, and felt my face

glowing all over. "Work, you know, in case you've forgotten what a job is."

He whistled, looking at me with admiration. "A job!" he exclaimed, and I knew he was happy for me. They're really glad if somebody gets work; they're not envious at all. It's something so big and important that there's no room left for ill feelings or jealousy. A job is given by Fate. Jerry may get one tomorrow, and he will tell me, expecting me to be glad about it, too.

But the reaction of my European friends is different. They hate you for getting a break; they try to smile, but their pale faces betray their real feelings. Why did he get the job and not I? they think. I, who worked for the Comédie Française; I, who played in Salzburg; I, who wrote a play that was shown on two hundred and twenty stages! And how quickly they console themselves: He only got it because his brother is a friend of the producer. He played poker with him. It's not *what* you know; it's *whom* you know! Who is his agent? they ask at once. Maybe I can get the job he has if I tell them how much more important I was in Europe....

That's why I have no European friends anymore. I stick to Eleanor and Jerry and their crowd. They have the right philosophy for this country. For them a job is earthly heaven; everything. A job is an excuse for anything. You can hop out of a woman's bed, and she will help you get away quickly, if there's a job calling you. You can break appointments, let people wait in the rain for hours, if you have to see someone about work. It's absolution. The Pope himself could not absolve your sins more completely than a job.

"Gosh," said Jerry, "I'm glad! I've got to tell Robin. She'll like it too!" He jumped out of the shower, but I stopped him.

"Don't embarrass her." I still had the old prejudice of aged Europe that the quite informal meeting between Robin and Jerry was something to be kept secret.

When boy meets girl and they like each other, there's not much fuss about it here. It's a kind of streamlined romance. I must get used to it, too. The rules are easy to understand even if you don't speak their language. The girl doesn't want to be forced; she hates to be urged. She wants to give the first hint. You can't go wrong if you wait. She wants to be courted, and in that way she doesn't differ from the European girl. She wants the usual flattery and devotion. But where a European girl has to be raped to preserve a clear conscience, these girls want freedom of mind and action. It takes away some of the "romance," which seems to be a great factor in every girl's life, but it simplifies things immensely.

Here they make everything plain. In France, we had to have twenty pieces of paper, stamped and recorded in different offices, to get one tool from the storeroom. Here you need only one slip, and you go get the tool yourself. I'm still amazed by their ingenuity in engineering: their heating systems in houses, operated by little push buttons; the hinges of their windows; the faucets of their water pipes; their simplified way of living; their markets, where you can buy meat and vegetables and salt and bread in a few minutes. In Europe, you'd have to shop in ten different places before you'd get a few things together.

I even have the impression that the faces of their young people are becoming streamlined, too. The high-school kids all look alike to me, boys and girls: the same straight figure—with some modifications on the boys' part, of course—long-legged, high cheek-boned, the eyes a little slant. It seems that the nation is changing back—or forth—to the original type of people who inhabited this continent. There's something in the air, in the salt of the earth, in the minerals of the water, in climate and wind, which changes the different types of human beings into a single one, adjusts itself to the requirements of life, and molds all of them into one nation, united not only by language and flag, but also by looks and reactions. I'm sure that in a few hundred years there will live in America a race not very different from the people the Pilgrims found and fought when they took possession of the land. Look at Jerry: tall and well-built, with narrow temples, strong chin, and sparsely cut lips. He was born here; has never left California. He doesn't even know how big the continent is. I know more about the land which is his than he does. But he is a type which can be found only here and nowhere else.

He had finished drying himself. He tossed the towel over one shoulder and rubbed hair tonic vigorously through his thick hair. He smiled up at me.

"They should have enough decency to go home in time. They go to bed easily, but how do you get 'em out again?"

"Your tough luck," I said airily. I was in love with him and everything else this morning.

"Let her sleep," I said, "and have breakfast with me at Schwab's." I felt like having breakfast twice this morning. The most beautiful moment of existence is between expectation and fulfillment. And I was going to drag this moment out as long as possible.

We tiptoed out of the room. Robin's blond hair, overflowing the white pillows, had not moved.

5

Joe Sherman looked his part. He was more than six feet tall. His slim, lithe body was bent forward—which cut him down to human size. His eyes were dark blue and enormous. A blond beard covered his chin. His cheeks were hollow, his forehead noble, his complexion pale. The model was obvious. He tried to look like someone who lived nearly two thousand years ago.

He spoke in a low and somehow melodious voice. I watched every movement while he talked to me, and tried to imagine this saint in bed with Eleanor. I shuddered. What did she see in him? Maybe his eyes would light up, his expression change; he'd lose that divine and demure expression; maybe he'd crawl out from behind his mask and become himself—if such a thing really existed.

It might be interesting for a girl to find out about him; I don't know about that, and I don't want to know. If I were a girl, I shouldn't be interested. I'd prefer Jerry with all his blandness, or someone like him. But I am wise enough to know that as long as you can't watch people in their bedrooms, behind closed doors, you have no right to judge them. What do you know about them? Only their fake outside; the act they put on for you. Surely they behave differently toward other people, adjust themselves to other personalities? To you, they may be friendly, harmless— to others, cunning and cruel. They may never betray any of their emotions to you, but might go to pieces in the presence of someone else. Sherman adjusted some papers before him. He was stalling for time. He wanted to have everything he was going to say to me clear in his mind.

When he began to talk, he changed. He looked at me for the first time after he had asked me to sit down, without giving me his hand. I looked into his eyes and discovered a lost, defenseless expression which begged me to be kind to him. If this attitude was intended, studied, it was clever of him, because it gave me a feeling of superiority. It added to his charm to make me believe I was worth much more than he.

But something else took possession of me and made me happy: it was the smell of the place. It breathed of the acid of the film laboratory and the sweet odor of film cement, mixed with the fragrance of celluloid. The air was saturated with waves of smells I loved.

"I got your name and address from M-G-M," Joe said, and cast his eyes down as if to beg forgiveness from heaven for his lie. "I found out that you're free—fortunately for me—and I supposed you'd have no objections to accepting a job. To tell you the truth, I don't know what it is. I got the order from a third party to employ a film cutter. As far as I know, it seems to be quite an interesting job. You're required to cut words from old films of Mr. Roger Niven. Your job is to find these words on the sound track and adjust them so that they can be recorded. I hope you understand." He looked up again and his eyes impressed me strangely. I saw pleading and submission in them.

"Certainly," I replied, "I understand. I have to construct a special dialogue, the words of which I have to cut out of old films. That's very clear—but would it not be much more convenient if Mr. Niven himself spoke that dialogue into the recording?"

With that advice I jeopardized my job. I always did silly things like that. I have lost almost all the chances in my life by being too clever.

"It's Mr. Marshall's wish to have it done the way I told you," Joe said in his melodious voice. "I got this order, and all I have to do is carry it out. The possibility you mentioned didn't even enter my mind, Mr. Bernet—Mr. Niven may not even be interested in doing the job. Why, he has said everything possible in his films. Here are more than a hundred thousand feet of film with his recorded voice. You could cut a novel from it. Why not carry out Mr. Marshall's order—which will satisfy him—and will give you employment!"

This was a rebuff. He was right. The boss is always right. You have to kowtow and take it. Or leave it.

"Did you say Mr. Marshall?" I asked, to make sure.

"You're going to meet him," Joe continued patiently. Marshall of the bloody lips!

"It's an extremely urgent job," Joe continued.

Well, that didn't surprise me. That's the motto of all film work. Everything they ask for has to be speeded up. Nothing on God's earth takes so much time hurrying things through as the film industry. The manuscript has to be delivered tomorrow, the shooting begins yesterday, the film has to be cut three weeks ago, and the preview has to be last year. The whole thing comes too late. Nobody ever has time; no time for himself, and no time for work, no time for anything but haste and nervousness and fear of finishing too late and losing the job.

"I'll do my best," I murmured, and waited for the most important announcement.

"How much was your salary at M-G-M?" Joe asked,

and put his thin white hands together. He knew it—
to hell with him. If he had really spoken to M-G-M, he
knew the color of the trunks I was wearing.

"I'd rather be paid for the whole job and have it left
to me to finish as soon as possible."

He liked the idea, this Jesuit, and nodded his Biblical
head.

"Mr. Marshall will pay you three hundred dollars
for the finished job, and one hundred in advance," he
said in a low voice. My heart stopped. I got seventy-
five dollars a week at M-G-M, and for a rush job Joe
offered me four whole weeks' salary! Eleanor had
tipped him off that I was broke. He was paying Eleanor
through me. I felt like a procurer getting his first
commission. But I hadn't the guts to tell Joe he was
paying me too much, and, coward that I am, I nodded
my consent. For a moment I felt an itch to tease him
and ask for more. He would raise the sum to bribe his
conscience. He had promised her to help me, and his
religion didn't permit him to go back on his word.

What dirty sins did he hide, what secret vices
tortured him, that he had to be so bigoted and humble?
I distrust kind people. If people are kind, they are
usually kind to themselves. Nobody is rich and strong
enough to be kind for kindness' sake alone. This man
wanted to be good to please the girl he loved and could
not get. It was nothing but a conversion of sensual
desire into deed. Otherwise, would he offer me three
hundred dollars for a job worth fifty? I detested him:
he tried to make peace between his soul and his
desires with a filthy three hundred bucks! I preferred
Marshall and his obvious, transparent cruelty; Joe,
that bag of dust and dirt, hiding behind his religion
and his saintly appearance, I despised. I hated him

because Eleanor didn't see through his thin disguise. I bet he never touched meat or drink; an oath would make him faint.

"Thanks," I said. "It's very good of you to offer me an advance. I'm rather short—odd you found that out so quickly!"

He took an envelope from the inside pocket of his linen jacket and carefully uncovered a hundred-dollar bill. Meticulously, he put it down and unfolded a receipt which he had properly written out in advance. To hurt him, I shoved the bill carelessly into my pocket, and with a flourish I wrote *merde* instead of my name on the receipt. I found a devilish pleasure in writing it. It looked like a signature.

"May I see the stuff now? I'd like to begin at once," I said, while he locked the receipt in his desk.

"Very well." He straightened up, a lithe, slightly bent saint, and opened the door of the next room. His coat was obviously cut by an expensive tailor. He spent money on his clothes! That did not fit his humility, but made his true character shine through the thin varnish of his fear of God.

We entered the cutting room, where an old-fashioned Moviola stood. The walls were covered with film boxes. Freshly sharpened pencils in a glass, a block of white paper ready to be used for notes, clothes hangers, linen covers for the chair—this organization was clean and orderly. Joe tried to keep the outside of his life in order because the inside was muddled up with desire, religion, and unhappiness.

"Mr. Marshall will be here soon," he said, and did not look up. "He'll give you any necessary information. Please understand that he's paying you, not I. I only rented the implements and the room to him. He gave me instructions to tell you that."

All this was very unusual and mysterious, as if I had to print banknotes or forge documents. I couldn't see anything sinister about cutting a film.

"Right-ho, okay," I said.

He left the room, walking noiselessly.

I sat down and took time out to be happy. Over there were the Moviola, scissors, cement, winder, film, and the heavenly smell of celluloid. And here was I, a working man—with money in my pocket. All the fear which had been haunting me night and day, holding its bony fingers on my throat and throttling me slowly and irresistibly, withered away. Why couldn't life always be like this; why was I always attacked by a paralyzing fear of tomorrow, of the coming night, of the next moment? Maybe I was not fit for life. Something was missing, had not been added to my blood when I was born. My whole defense mechanism against the hardships of life consists of one first line, without reserves. I've always known I would die a strange death; that I wouldn't die in bed. I have prepared myself for it because I have been aware of it since I was ten.

I remember Madame Dumanceau, my mother's trusted friend, who was a fortuneteller. Mother believed in her religiously. And very clearly I see this queer old woman advising my mother, looking at dirty, greasy cards, telling her about the future. "After your forty-second birthday, you needn't walk anymore," Madame Dumanceau had said, and had smiled kindly at her. I still see her dark and rather intelligent eyes as she told mother this prophecy. Of course, mother believed she'd be so rich she would ride in a coach all the time. She died shortly after her forty-second birthday. "And this little boy," Madame Dumanceau had said, after laying out the cards for me, "well—I can't see anything for him after he's thirty—" and she looked at me rather curiously. I didn't understand; I was too young. But later on, when I thought about it, I knew she meant I was to die before my thirtieth birthday. That old hag had poisoned my mind for many years, and still, at thirty-four, fear sits on my neck and throttles me.

I sometimes wonder why I have gone through all this trouble instead of finishing the nightmare in a painless and pleasant fashion. Only curiosity has given me the strength to live. I must know what will come next; which is as good reason as any. I feel it is a very good and almost foolproof one. There seems to be no sense in life. Get all the fun you can and be done with it. If you come across a nice piece of meat, eat it yourself.

In America, people live simple, uncomplicated lives. They live only for the moment; there's no haunting fear in their eyes; they face life and live it calmly, even when they are in bigger jams than I. Take Jerry, for example. What will happen to him when he gets older? He has never thought of that. He wants a job very badly. They all want jobs to live life as they want it. They want money in their pockets, but they rarely save. A job—that's the assurance of being able to buy gasoline for the car and alcohol for the other mechanism; to treat a girl to dinner; to have the right to sleep with her afterwards; to make the first payment on the radio, the car, a dress, on love, and to produce babies on the part-payment system.

They don't take death very seriously either. They have more resistance. They don't make a fuss about anything. Because they don't fear life, they're not afraid to die; they don't even think of it. Everything is casual and must be treated that way. They don't like to hear about the troubles of their fellow men. They don't like to reveal their own, and if they are compelled to, they do it with a laugh. They always carry a smile on their lips and they expect it from others.

That's one reason why I stand outside their world. Two thousand years of church history in Europe has impressed us with the importance of life and death, has made living difficult, and dying fearful. Unconscious fear of Hell and Purgatory and Judgment Day overshadows our happiness. To me, everything is tragic. It's in my blood. But here there is nothing tragic enough to bother people. They want to avoid boredom—that's their main objective. Look at their books and pictures, which emphasize that cruelty can be amusing and death can be a thrill—if you yourself are not the victim, of course. They haven't the cinders of a medieval tradition in their souls. But despite all their directness and bluntness, they're kind. Because they like to live without unnecessary difficulties, they help each other in every way. That creates a sociability without which life would not pass so smoothly.

"Mr. Bernet," a voice behind me said. It was Mrs. Sherman, the woman Joe had brought from France. She had pronounced the name correctly. She looked at me with dark, Latin eyes; her hair was very platinum. I disliked her expression at once. She was about forty. Although she seemed to have given up trying to look attractive, she still had designs on pleasure. Too many designs, it seemed to me. She was somewhat voluptuous, not bad between belly and throat, but her frustration made her ugly. I knew this type very well. She could have been a hated concierge in Neuilly. There was only one way to make friends with women like her: to flatter her conceit. At once I jumped up and bowed deeply. My European upbringing permitted me to be overpolite. They laugh at an American who does this stuff, but they always expect a Frenchman to behave like D'Artagnan and the Three Musketeers. And she had been in America long enough to appreciate my contortions.

"You're Mr. Bernet," she said, and knew that I was, scrutinizing me. But I was on my guard. She was only too ready to turn all her accumulated hate and disgust against me if I only flicked an eye. I think she had never had enough from life; had never been satisfied for a minute. She was the type who would get thirstier as she drank. She was too much for Joe, and that's why he tried to hide behind his holiness, which sprang from the desire to escape her, mentally and physically. I suddenly understood Joe and his beard, his way of talking and his kindness. I suffered with him when I looked at her.

"At your service, Madame." I smiled. She melted a little. Evidently she liked anything in trousers, but I scored one point above the average.

"Did Mr. Sherman give you that job? Where does he know you from? How much is he paying you?" she asked in a breathless way, without giving me a chance to answer.

"He got my name from M-G-M, and Mr. Marshall takes care of the financial end. I know Mr. Marshall very intimately. He's a good friend of mine and was very pleased to give me the job."

I lied to her like an unfaithful husband. It gave me a devilish pleasure to hoax her, and look honest and modest at the same time. But she did not seem to be convinced. She had that awful, tiresome sixth sense unhappy women sometimes possess for difficulties, secrecies and excuses. She divined that something was wrong about me and tried to find out what it was. It was Eleanor, but Mrs. Sherman didn't know how to arrive at that conclusion.

She said: "Mr. Marshall just telephoned he will be here presently." She still spoke English with a heavy French accent, as I do—but we both spoke English. French would have indicated too much intimacy.

I smiled, and looked at her breasts to make her happy. She was the kind of woman one could get money from; it would satisfy her motherly instinct to help poor boys sail around the sharp cliffs of life, if she got something personal in exchange. She was the type who has to have children. Without an outlet for her fertility, she was bound to be bitter and dissatisfied. I suddenly had the whim to give Joe and Eleanor a very good reason for a divorce. That shouldn't be difficult. Joe would revert back to his true self; Eleanor would see to that. He would shed all his holiness and inhibitions like a snakeskin.

"Are these the films?" I asked, walking toward her, pointing at the obvious inscriptions on the boxes. She stared at me, and quite casually my elbow touched her soft breast for a moment. She didn't move; she was stone; nothing in her face betrayed her feelings. I grabbed one box, stepping very close to her. I felt the warmth and softness of her ripe body. She was repulsive in her cowlike acquiescence. I suddenly was disgusted and stepped back, and lost all my good intentions of helping Eleanor. Mrs. Sherman had not said a word. She turned around and left the room, slamming the door.

I suddenly felt uneasy. She was incalculable. What would she do next? Would she put poison in my coffee, or would I find her at home in my bed? What a life poor Joe must have at her side. So much hate and viciousness were piled up in her, looking for escape, that she was as dangerous as a barrel of TNT. A few months in a soldiers' brothel might help her a lot. The safest thing was to kill her off without much ado. She left such a fog of ugly personality in the room that I opened the window.

I took the hundred-dollar bill out of my pocket and looked at it. It was genuine. I straightened it out and put it in my leather folder as carefully as Joe had taken it from the envelope. When I looked up I saw Marshall watching me—me and the bill. Why the hell did he have to sneak in like that?

"Hello," I said quite casually, opened a film box, took out the reel and looked at it. He closed the door without turning around.

"I didn't expect to find you here," he said. His voice was hoarse from drinking.

"No? Whom did you expect?" I had the hundred bucks safely in my pocket, and a promise of the rest. He had to pay me, even if somebody else did the job. Obviously he felt ill at ease.

He asked: "Can you cut a film?"

I said: "I have thought so for the last eight years— maybe I'm wrong."

He pondered for a moment. "Funny to see you here."

"It's not so funny. There're not many good people out of a job. Joe seemed to be delighted at finding that I was available."

I was bold for my three hundred.

"It's a special job," he said, and took a sheet of paper from his pocket, "and an urgent one."

"I know all about it," I replied curtly.

He seemed startled but made up his mind at once.

"What the hell—why not?" he said incoherently, and slammed the paper on the table. "Look here, that's the dialogue I want you to find among the film."

I picked up the paper and began to read carefully. It didn't make much sense to me.

—Certainly—you can have it. If you let me play in your next film, and give me billing before you . . .

That was one line.

—I don't care if you know about my affairs. I like to eat at home, but the restaurant has its advantages too. All right, I haven't been faithful, if you call it that. But how are you going to prove it? The jury wants proof!

And it went on like that, making no sense at all. My mind was blank. I looked at him quizzically. "I don't follow—what's this all about?"

Marshall's ugly face was motionless. He took his handkerchief and cleaned his lips. I turned my eyes away.

"I'm not paying you to understand; I'm paying you to do the work." Well, Joe had warned me.

"But how can I find these words—for example, here's the word 'affairs.' It might not be among all those miles of sound track . . ."

"If you can't find it, take another word for it, a substitute. I thought you were clever. If you can't do the job, just forget about it!" His frozen eyes glittered, unfriendly. I didn't like them.

"All right, I'll do everything possible. You want approximately this dialogue—if I understand rightly."

"You do!"

That was that. I took a film reel out of a tin box and ran it through the Moviola, switching on the current. The lamps heated up and the dialogue came hollow through the speaker.

It was the fourth reel of "The Vagabond from Broadway," an old film of Roger Niven's, but not his best. I listened to the sound, finger on the switch.

"Here it is," I said impressively.

"What?" Marshall was visibly startled by my efficiency. I did my best to show off, increasing the volume of the speaker, raising the sound to a deafening noise, running the film and the voices backwards. It was quite a show.

"The words 'all right' which we needed—here it says, 'All right, my sweetheart; I'll be back in time.' I'll just cut out 'all right' and separate it."

I stopped the motor and marked the track, took the scissors and cut out the sound, wrote "all right" on a sheet, put the cut film on it, pasted the ends of the celluloid together with cement, and was extremely busy for a couple of minutes.

I felt great, convincing Marshall what an expert he had hired.

When I looked at him, I saw that he wasn't at all impressed.

"You can do more with much less fuss," he said dryly. "Sherman has dialogue sheets on all the films. Mark the words and cut them out. That's all I need. I'll be here tomorrow to see how much you've done. Good day."

Out he went without giving me so much as a glance. There I was, alone with the Moviola and dusty film boxes. I sat down. The feeling of adventure which I had had since Joe called me floated away from me.

But still the positive fact of the hundred-dollar bill in my pocket remained. Again I read the dialogue sheet. The Hays office wouldn't pass it, I was sure of that. Marshall might use it for a private film to show to his friends, or for a practical joke. They're great for practical jokes; it's part of their existence.

I tried to guess the missing dialogue lines. Obviously it concerned a talk between husband and wife about marriage difficulties. I suddenly remembered that Roger Niven was Marjorie Dean's husband. But that didn't give me much of a clue. Their marriage was an exhibition piece: the "perfect married couple," the *pièce de résistance* and pride of Hollywood. Niven was well liked by everyone, very cultured, no longer young. He drank, like most successful Hollywood people. Marjorie Dean was a beautiful woman in her late twenties. Both were highly intelligent, compared to the average actor. I think they had been married for more than four years. This is a kind of record, something to be proud of.

He had been married four times before, but he wasn't a Bluebeard—he was just unlucky. Any man who had been divorced four times should be divorced again, according to the law of repetition and permutation. It may not even have been his fault. His fate was to fall for the type of woman who unfailingly will divorce him later on. If he had been born with a penchant for the species which marries only once, he would have stuck to his first wife. But, unfortunately, he fell for the other extreme, and that explains his collection of marriage licenses.

The door opened with a thud and Mrs. Sherman entered. I hadn't been wrong about her. A strange change had come over her. Her hair was properly combed; it wasn't bad—too platinum, but thick. She had fastened it into a knot which covered the white, fat flesh of her neck. Her mouth was painted bright red, but she didn't know enough about make-up to form her lips properly. Crude colors covered the rest of her face. She was ready for the word "go." To me, she looked even more hideous than before; but in her eyes it was a great improvement. She had even changed the spotty dress for a clean light one which showed her figure too much. She was more cowlike than ever. I appreciated her going to so much trouble to make herself presentable to me, and smiled at her affectionately. She savored my improper compliment like a precious liqueur. She certainly wasn't spoiled by too many tributes to her charm.

I had developed a certain technique, a clever trick to cut out ill feelings. If I don't like someone, I hypnotize myself into the belief that something about him or her is lovable: the mouth, the forehead, or a way of talking, or anything I can pick out without being too disillusioned. And I show a genuine liking, which is contagious. My opponent always begins to like me. And now my trick had worked again. Mrs. Sherman was convinced at this moment that she was beautiful.

"Here's the dialogue sheets of the films." She put down a pile of papers. "Don't lose them; we have no copies."

She forced herself to be hard, but a certain softness shone through her voice. That irritated her. She didn't want me to be aware of it, but she couldn't suppress it. It was one of her rare moments of kindness, perhaps the only one.

"You're extremely kind to me, Mrs. Sherman." My

voice was sugarcoated. You couldn't overdo it with her; she was prepared to swallow the smallest flattery. I began to smear it on as thick as possible. "I really don't know why you bother with it. Isn't it Mr. Sherman's job to see to it? I'm not very experienced, Mrs. Sherman. I hope you won't mind my turning to you in case I need advice. I'm sure I can't manage this job without your kind help!"

I felt like spitting at myself, but she swallowed my flattery hook, line, sinker and pole. Her dark eyes looked as if she were prepared to rape me, and I sent a quick prayer to heaven for a miracle to save me. It came: Joe entered. If he saw the change in his wife he was able to hide his reactions. He held his white hands together; his pious head was bent.

"Mr. Marshall spoke to me again, Mr. Bernet," he said, ignoring her. She could have been thin air as far as he was concerned. "Mr. Marshall again asked me to have the job finished quickly; Tomorrow he'll send you a sound track which you'll kindly incorporate. I assume he told you all about it."

He slowly turned his big, blue eyes on me, and again they seemed to beg for help and understanding.

"I'm thoroughly informed," I said. There was a bond between us, an instinctive front against that painted, warlike woman. She sensed it at once and ran out of the room, slamming the door.

Joe didn't move, but his suffering was tangible. It was like a solid substance in this room that smelled of film cement and celluloid.

"Everything has its solution and end. We have only to wait and to be patient. So often I've stood with my back against the wall and thought there was no way out—but suddenly it opened. And I was saved." I said all these beautiful words quietly, and felt like a saint. It didn't even sound wrong to me when I said it.

Joe grasped the meaning of my priestly speech and left his shell for a moment.

"You are a very kind man, Mr. Bernet," he said in a soft voice that stabbed through my heart.

Now I understood Eleanor's liking for Joe, and, strangely enough, it didn't make me jealous at all. On the contrary, I had a quaint feeling of contentment and happiness.

6

That night I went home early. I bathed, shaved, changed, and walked around naked for half an hour whistling, so full of pep that I was astonished at myself. I was going to call for Eleanor at eight and we were to have a drink and dinner together at the Beachcomber's.

I was glad to see her again. It was something more than just gladness; it was something I hadn't felt for a long time; something burning when I thought of her. I wondered if it was produced by a physiological condition—sexual abstinence—which makes you see Venus in every woman. No—it was something more. I felt happy. I wanted to laugh for no reason. How could I be in love with a little kid like her? It was absurd! But still, when I thought of her, that funny burning feeling crept back at once.

I didn't even have a pornographic book at hand to help me get rid of that indisposition which was softening me toward the whole world. What I dislike most is to feel approachable and easy. Anyhow, it didn't do me any harm; I left it at that and became really excited about going to her. Often I caught myself thinking about her. I had really begun to care for her. I knew only too well that I was going to be disappointed, but even this certainty did not make any difference in my feelings toward her. And so I arrived too early, against my better judgment.

She lived in a bungalow off Melrose Avenue. It was one of those sinister-looking buildings which they move away at night when the owner feels he wants a new view from his window in the morning.

These bungalows are comparatively big. Eleanor's had nine rooms. What she did with them I don't know. She had a rather old dog, half blind, with no charms whatsoever, not even devotion to her. He was a French bull terrier. I disliked him at once, and our dislike was mutual. But I had a good reason for my antipathy; he stank.

I met Mother. Mother was an interesting and kind soul. Mother liked a little swig from time to time, and that made her quite sympathetic. She was a little woman, around fifty, brittle as if the desert wind had dried the juice out of her bones. She was a chain smoker. When from time to time her heart gave her trouble, she cut down on cigarettes and took only one or two drinks extra. She greeted me heartily, knowing everything about me. Eleanor had given me a nice build-up.

Eleanor was, like any other woman on earth you call for, not ready. She called from the bathroom that she'd be out in a minute; I should have a drink in the meantime.

Well, I had a couple or more, and talked to Mother. I felt so happy that I was afraid. To be happy leaves you wide open to attack.

Mother was sitting in an overstuffed chair, ogling me in a maternal way, taking the measure of my earning capacity and my many other manly virtues, chatting gaily, cutting the minutes into seconds. Her chatter induced me to take another stiff drink. She didn't mind. Then she went on to reminisce, thoroughly enjoying it. She had been a barmaid in a mining town up in Idaho, way up in the mountains. She still had a longing to go back there.

It must have been quite a place! Time had stood still there since the eighties, and people were still running around with six-shooters. Modern times hadn't licked them yet.

She found it very natural that I should take her daughter out. In Europe it would have happened in quite another way, and much more formally. If a man calls for a girl at her home, it's considered a very definite step toward the goal of marriage. But here, where the kiss on the doorstep is the established method of saying good night and means no more than a handshake, mothers see young men enter their houses whom they never expect to meet again.

This is all much more natural than the European way. It takes the curse off the relationship between the boy and the girl's mother. Mother takes it for granted that her daughter will have some fun before she is tied to a dull marriage.

Eleanor came out from behind the curtain which shut off the living room. She looked fresh and very lovely. Her skin, which she had inherited from her English grandmother, was transparent. Her blond hair—from some Norwegian ancestor—shone like a halo, and she had the trim little figure of a Latin ingénue, her grandfather having been a Frenchman. All together, she was of pure, undiluted American blood.

"Hello, Pierre," she said, and knew exactly what impression she had made on me. You can see that in their eyes. They have a special look which disappears only after you've paid the homage they are dying to hear.

"God, you're beautiful—but I'm sure someone has told you that before!" I took Mrs. Marr's daughter in my arms and kissed her carefully, so as not to disarrange any part of her exterior. I did it quite impulsively—my reaction to her beauty. And how it pleased her! She took my arm and dragged me toward the door. I kissed the old lady's hand and gave the dog a secret kick. The dog howled. Now he, too, had a reason.

"Shut up, Fluffy!" Eleanor said. "It's strange that he doesn't like you. I don't know why. He likes all my other friends."

But I kept my opinion of the dog for a more appropriate time.

We drove my little bus toward the Beachcomber's. I was prepared to spend ten bucks, and I was going to do it in style. Eleanor sat very close to me, as was right. You have only to glance into a car to know at once by the distance between driver and passenger how much they are in love with each other.

We rolled along Highland Avenue. My car was my sanctuary, Eleanor being a part of it. I felt like one of the high-school kids who speed along in jalopies with no mudguards, accompanied by their highly painted young ladies. Indians on the warpath!

I wished I could be young again, but here in America,

life is made so easy, and the casual way of existence gives you more chances to concentrate on the major problems of life. But the young people who know nothing but this cannot imagine how difficult it will be afterwards; a pity that youth is wasted on children! They lack the appreciation which only experience can give. They don't enjoy it as I did at just that moment, driving Eleanor to the Beachcomber's. Things in life are exciting only when they are out of the ordinary. And what I did was certainly ordinary to young people—driving along and feeling content for no reason at all.

"Why are you driving so slowly?" Eleanor asked. She moved still closer, if that were possible without crawling onto my lap.

"Three guesses," I said, and put my arm around her waist.

"You shouldn't make love to me." She was quite alarmed. She didn't trust herself. I drove along in silence.

"Happy?" she asked. Her voice was kind. She was aware of the resistance she put up and tried to make everything agreeable.

I looked straight ahead. She was slightly irritated. I knew what ailed her. Why couldn't I be like all her other friends? Why was I so possessive in everything? She would have been happy if I were simply her friend, nothing more....

But I wonder if she would still have been interested in me. She always expected me to be super-intelligent, to say clever things, to think about every sentence before I spoke. She would never have forgiven me if I had indulged in utter nonsense. That was for her gang. She wanted me to be special, like a crossbreed between

Pythia and Socrates. Her belief that I was very clever shifted me right outside her normal sphere of life.

"Are we going to the Beachcomber's?" she asked, quite anxiously. I smiled and nodded, and she seemed to be relieved for some obscure reason.

We stopped at the parking lot, and Eleanor waited until I went around the car to open the door and help her out. She put her full weight on my arm. She found this little ceremony very gentlemanly and quite unusual, and it pleased her. They're not much spoiled by courtesy here. I held her very close for a fraction of a second.

Herbert, the manager, was happy to see us. He was a tall fellow in white trousers who tried to look very tropical despite the slight handicap of being Norwegian.

"Hello, Pierre," he said, slapping my shoulder. "I'm still reserving the little table for you."

The place was crowded, as usual, the dark-blue night sky looked through the roof of bamboo leaves, and a Hawaiian orchestra played soft love songs. A faint fragrance of rum hung in the warm air and made the people susceptible to a lot of things.

Herbert, walking along with me, whispered in my ear. He always did it when I came with a girl he hadn't seen me with before.

"I'll make the evening easy for you," he said, with his hard Norwegian pronunciation. That meant he was going to put more rum in my lady's glass.

He was full of appreciation for Eleanor's beauty, and I felt very proud, because every man finds his girl extremely exquisite as soon as his friends remind him. In fact, many men have to be told about the beauty of the women they go with before they realize it at all.

We ordered some poison called Zombi, which allegedly consists of five ounces of different rums, to which a touch of absinthe is added. Eleanor went off to the ladies' room, returned, frigidly disregarding all the appraising eyes which followed her highly gaited walk. She looked as beautiful as a girl kept by a producer who makes over five thousand a week. I definitely made up my mind to do something about her, Joe or no Joe!

She looked toward the door and questioned me slyly: "It's my evening, isn't it?" I said "Yes" and understood why a second later. Emily was coming along—Emily with the dark beautiful eyes and the mouth which looked as if she disliked men.

"Did you invite her?" I asked, before Emily was within hearing distance.

"Certainly, you wolf!" She gave Emily her hand. "Hello, Emily. Where is Connie? And why didn't you bring Virginia?"

"Hello, Pierre!" Emily said. A sudden light in her dark eyes made her whole face shine. "Oh—the girls will be here a little later . . ."

Passing her the drink a Hawaiian boy had just brought me, I smiled and began flirting with her.

"I must tell you something, Emily, I just found out," I said casually. "Eleanor is a coward! I'm really glad you came, because I like your eyes and everything above and below them. But Eleanor didn't call you out of friendship. She is just jittery! That's the reason! She called on you for help; she doesn't trust herself, not even here among this crowd; she's afraid I'll rape her right here on top of the table in front of all the nice people. That's why you, Virginia, Connie and their husbands have to butt in."

"Gee—on top of a table—that must be a strange feeling," Emily said and looked bewildered. She did that expression quite well.

Eleanor was shaken. She obviously wasn't sure why she had arranged for Emily and Virginia to come, but having been told the reason, and suddenly becoming aware of it, she was upset and offended.

"You're a coward," I said and raised my glass. "To your missing courage, coward!" I drank. She didn't touch her glass.

"You're horrid," she said. Her eyes were dark with rage. "Joe would never say a thing like that!"

The name hit me. It must have shown in my face. Her only defense was to call on Joe or me for help. Having to fight me, she called for Joe. She was hiding her own weakness behind his name as he hid behind his funny religion.

I bent toward Emily and took her small, cool hand in mine, trying to make Eleanor jealous. "Eleanor is afraid I will make her tight and use her intoxication to talk about love, telling her how much I like her. I might even go so far as to persuade her to come to my room. Just think! She is a tottering leaf on the tree of desire—and she knows it. That's why she called her bodyguard out: you, Virginia, Connie.... To hell with Eleanor! Let's drink to you—" I gulped the rest of my drink down. Emily was alarmed. She didn't know how to act; she didn't even understand me. She thought we had been quarreling and frantically searched for the right words.

"Don't bother," Eleanor said. "He's just trying out one of his funny speeches on you. I often wonder if he knows what he says. But he's quite nice. He could even be a good friend, but something beastly in him prevents it. Have a drink and shut up." Putting her hand in mine, she asked for forgiveness. She was suffering. She tried to keep me among her friends, and I made it difficult for her, exposing her little tricks.

"Now I'm ready for a double Zombi," Emily said, recovering from her shock. "Can't you behave like normal people, both of you? I don't know what you're talking about. Why don't you both go home and get it over with?" She was a good sport.

These girls are much more faithful to each other than a man can ever be to a woman. She knew that Eleanor was attached to me and she wouldn't have cut in for anything in the world. I was "taboo" for all the girls of Eleanor's circle, and only if Eleanor went out with someone else, officially casting me off, would I have a chance to approach one of the other girls.

Five minutes later Virginia arrived, talkative and starved as usual, and Connie came a minute later. They wanted only one drink, and it took a lot of persuasion to force them to have another one. They, too, extended their friendship and kindness to me. Otherwise they would have been a rather expensive and thirsty little crowd, quite cunning in making strangers pay without giving anything in return but a promising smile.

We didn't stay very long because Virginia expected her husband to come home. He was a prop man at Paramount; Connie's husband, a swing at Goldwyn's. But Eleanor decided what to do: she invited all of them for dinner at my place. I had to buy the food. And why not get a bottle of whisky, too? It was cheaper than spending big dough on expensive liquor in bars.

Joyfully, Eleanor took my arm as if she had found the ideal way to spend the evening pleasantly. She had something on her mind. She wanted to go to my apartment, but she didn't want to be there alone. To go up there at night was a promise in itself and she wanted to avoid that. But still, she wanted to be there.

"Do you play chess?" I asked her.

"No—why?" she asked, putting on her most unapproachable expression as we left the place.

"Because you think many moves ahead."

"I want to be alone with you afterwards," she said plainly. It made my heart stop.

7

The gang left me after midnight. Sensing drink and food, Jerry arrived with the punctuality of an eclipse. He came in just as Connie was putting the bacon on the stove. The bottle of whisky was finished in a hurry, but Jerry produced some bourbon. After they had left, not a crumb of anything to eat could be found in my place. A mouse would have starved to death.

Virginia and Connie had washed the dishes and glasses. Virginia's husband, Martin, had a row with her because Virginia had flirted unnecessarily with Jerry, and Jerry had promptly tried to date her. She was to blame for it because she had given him every reason to ask. But after I had tipped off Jerry that I wanted to be alone with Eleanor, he proved his outstanding organizational ability and cleared the apartment of all my guests without offending them, just by saying bluntly that I wanted to be alone. They departed at once, assuring me they had had a very pleasant evening.

Connie invited me to her birthday shower, hinting

she needed stockings urgently. Little Emily hated to leave. She had no work to do next morning and wanted to talk to someone. She was not tired, she said. She felt lost. Jerry was not interested in her; she was not spoiled enough for his taste. His meat was girls of easy virtue who didn't ask him for money. That seemed to him a supreme demonstration of real love. A tart giving something for nothing was like a kind-hearted shop-owner giving away his goods to people who were passing by. It showed a striking appreciation of his male qualities. Young girls might stay with him out of politeness, but that didn't inflate his ego.

He didn't like Emily. He wouldn't have been successful, either, and he knew it. He boasted once that no woman he ever really wanted had refused him. But he added truthfully that he wouldn't try to become chief engineer at Chrysler's; he would never ask for a job he was sure not to get. He played safe. It was very safe with girls like Robin, whose heart was so starved that she mistook Jerry's brutality for love.

I sat down to smoke while Eleanor very busily emptied the ashtrays and opened the windows for a moment to get the atmosphere of her friends out. She closed the windows again, drew the curtains, switched out the lights and left a small table lamp burning behind the writing desk. It shone from afar and cast our shadows in immense proportions over the walls.

I got up and took the bed out of the cupboard. It came down with a dull thump.

She stopped on her way from the kitchen.

"Don't," she said firmly. I paid no attention to her, and stretched myself on the bed comfortably, indicating that it was much more agreeable to lie down than to sit up in those decrepit chairs of mine. I smoked and waited, and watched my hand forming gigantic silhouettes on the ceiling. Eleanor finally came to me and sat on the edge of the bed beside me and we smoked our cigarettes silently.

"Would you mind if I go to bed?" I asked her. "I want to be comfortable for once in my life."

She thought she would be much safer with me in a weak position—I in pajamas and she dressed—so she nodded. I went to the bathroom and changed quickly. My heart thudded. I shaved hurriedly with my electric razor and returned, went back to bed, took the cigarette out of her hand and smoked. The mouthpiece was red with lipstick and smelled like vanilla.

"Go on—shoot," I said, looking at her. Her face was deadly serious, her straight little nose had a small shiny spot, her eyes were deep and filled with an emotion I couldn't understand at all. She wasn't thinking of me, but I was prepared for anything.

"May I kiss you once before I get an inferiority complex?" I asked her. She nodded, her face retaining its serious expression. She bent down, her lips cool. I kissed her. There was no resistance at all. But no emotion, either. I fell back, putting her cigarette between my lips again.

"What do you think of Joe?" she asked. I knew that question would come up. I was expecting it, but it hurt me even in spite of my foresight.

"You're a cold-hearted fish with ice water in your veins, or you wouldn't ask me a question like that now," I said quietly. I didn't understand her race, her breed, her nature. Where else in the world would a girl sit on the bed of a man who she knew was in love with her, and question him about her real lover? But she wasn't aware of her cruelty. She was an egotist through and through. Nothing mattered but her own life and love. For her, I was less than a leaf blown by a casual wind across her feet. I was merely someone she could talk to about Joe.

"You met him," she said simply, "and you know about human nature. You must tell me. I have to know!" Prepared for the worst, she looked at me with a curious shine in her eyes. She had made up her mind about him and all she wanted was to hear her own opinion from someone else.

"All right," I said, "I'll tell you the truth. I think you're making a mistake."

I closed my eyes and thought of Joe and suddenly I felt a great pity for him. It was surely the alcohol that produced that strange emotion. I couldn't figure out why I didn't trample him to the ground; it was certainly to my own disadvantage to help him.

"I don't think you're strong enough to get that sham holiness out of him. It doesn't belong to him; he wasn't born with it. It's nothing but a defense against his wife, and he'll do the same with you if he doesn't find in you what he's expecting. You're taking a big chance and you know it. You know it so well that you'll listen only to what you want to hear. Anything else would enter one of your little ears and leave through the other without touching your brain."

She looked at me with big eyes; her mouth was curled in a smile which indicated that my doubt about her strength to save him could not touch her. Then I knew definitely that I had lost for good. I had lost her without even having conquered her.

I realized I loved her; I realized it for the first time, and it made me desperate. I was a pig, a scoundrel, a half-wit, who cared for nothing but his own pleasure;

my ego had grown with a few petty successes and I had overlooked the fact that other people, too, have feelings and reactions. I had lost the ability of elastic youth to find new companions easily, to make new friends, and to live with them without friction. I had lost the quality of making real friends. I wanted only myself. I was egotistical and callous; I wasn't even able to win such a trusting, straight little soul like Eleanor.

I had spoiled everything—not wise enough to wait, too impatient to let feelings grow. I behaved like a goat in a beautiful garden, trampling to pieces what I couldn't swallow.

"You see," I said, and she looked up; I think my voice had changed, "you took on a big job to get close to Joe's soul. He really seems to have one. But who knows for sure? It's possible that you'd be very happy with him. But don't ask my opinion. I haven't enough brains to figure that out. And besides, I have enough egotism to deny it, because I'm in love with you myself, and I don't want to give you up. I know I have to, because there's no chance for me, and I've just realized it."

She nodded, listening to me like a schoolgirl to a teacher who was infallible in her eyes.

"If he didn't have a wife, everything would be all right. I'm certain of it. He must get rid of her, and soon! And if he has not enough guts to do it himself, I'll help him—and you at the same time. That's a promise!"

I felt so rotten that I had to close my eyes. I had promised something in which I didn't believe and which I couldn't fulfill anyhow. I felt exhausted.

She put her hand on my forehead and was lying down beside me, her other hand under her hair. The warmth of her body came through the linen of the bed. Here she was. I had only to stretch out my hands—but I knew it would do no good. For the first time in my life I was careful not to destroy what was growing slowly. It was like a timid fire burning under wet wood which would go out if a gust of wind hit it. She rolled onto her side and put her cool face close to mine, and I felt her tears running down my cheeks. I didn't breathe. I waited while her tears kept running, silently, out of control.

"Be patient, Eleanor," I said, "you must . . . and forgive me if I was unkind to you. Everything will be all right—you know that, don't you? You know it deep in your heart; otherwise you couldn't carry on. We all know that—or we wouldn't have the strength to live. You are in love—and that's the only time life is worth living. Then why do you cry? Be happy about it. He is not free now but he will be. He loves you, too. Is there any imaginable reason to be sad? I'm going to help you—thoroughly, even if I have to murder that old bitch to clear the way for you. You see—to be truthful—I haven't done many good deeds in my life. To be very frank, I haven't done any! My nature revolts when I try to be kind. But this time you have my promise! I will do anything for you, and there are things I can do if I want to!"

I supported myself on my hands and looked down at her, took the edge of the pillow and carefully dried her eyes.

"Please don't cry anymore," I said, and smiled.

She closed her eyes, and there was a tear lingering in the corner of her mouth. I picked it up with my little finger. I wanted to kiss her, but she might not have understood me.

"You're very kind to me, Pierre," she said, "and I am not kind to you. I know it—but what can I do?"

"I'll take you home," I said, in a loud voice, to cut the whole mood to pieces. I did it purposely to bring her back to herself. "Do you know that I kicked your poor dog today to make him growl? He had a damn good reason to be sore at me!"

I got up, put on my dressing gown and slippers.

"Fluffy?" She was really shocked, which was what I wanted. "What did you do to poor Fluffy?"

"I kicked him because he stank!" I took my overcoat and hat. She sat up, covering her face for a moment, but she controlled herself perfectly. All these girls go through a hard school and are used to keeping themselves under control. They never let themselves go. That's the result of their dance training and their work. When they need it, they all have balance, a strong will, equilibrium.

"Let's go," she said. She got up, without bothering about her make-up. "You needn't take me home. I'll take a taxi."

I put my arm around her shoulders, pressed her to me, and didn't say a word. We went downstairs. The man at the reception desk, who was well trained, didn't look up.

Silently, we drove to her house. I walked up with her, took the key out of her hand and unlocked the door. She stood on the stairs, as tall as I. Her face shone pale and childlike in the yellow glow of the street light. There was no sound whatsoever. It was the hour between night and morning, when one day has passed and the new one is just taking its first breath. Even the distant rumble of cars had ceased.

She kissed me with cold lips.

"You're kind, Pierre," she said. I heard tears in her voice again. Quickly she turned and closed the door.

I went back to my car. My steps sounded loud on the granite flags of the garden path. I started the car. The night was very cool. I shivered. I knew it was the most beautiful day of my life. Someone had cried—for me.

8

"Righteousness exalteth a people," Solomon says. And here in Los Angeles, Solomon's words, translated from Hebrew into Greek into Latin into English, is just the right motto for the town hall, which is called by cynical people: "The Temple of Graft."

Well, nobody ever tried to bribe me. If I had something worth paying a bribe for, I'd sell it. Just once in my life I'd like to get something for nothing. What a beautiful feeling it must be to get paid without working for it, to earn money by only closing one eye or both. It lifted me up, reading Solomon's beautiful words, spoken by a king who knew what he was talking about. And here they were, chiseled into stone, adorning the entrance of a million-dollar building.

You enter the big hall, walk over the copper bas-relief of a ship, and there are dozens of elevators waiting for you. A man with a kind of castanet directs them. I envy him his job. To be clad in a uniform, to look very efficient and to be paid for making a noise with a rattle is something to be proud of. You have to be born with the knack for a job like this; and when you finally die, honored and respectable, your funeral paid for by the town, you can truthfully say: "I didn't live a useless life. I rattled!"

"Where's the Superior Court?" I asked the rattler.

"Eight," he said cryptically, and made his well-rewarded noise.

The Tower express took me up in no time. There I was, standing in a long corridor. Court was in session and a great number of people were waiting. Along the wall stood a row of chairs like those in a cinema, with old-fashioned wrought-iron backs. Here the town saved money, buying its stuff from a used-furniture dealer.

I waited, looking around. I had enough time on my hands again. Days ago I had completed my job, and every minute that passed without making me feel useless enlarged my life.

The atmosphere was rather depressing. In a place where people fight for happiness, for money, for their lives, you always feel fear and anxiety hanging in the air like a tangible substance. Fear materializes; it is contagious; it affects other people. I became rather uneasy, walking along the corridor, waiting for His Honor, Judge Brentford.

I passed the private conference room, with panels of frosted glass, furnished with a round table and easy chairs. Next came a press room and some staircases for people who wanted to leave the place in a hurry.

I stepped into the courtroom and sat down in the last row among the others who were watching and enjoying other people's troubles, glad that this time it was not they who were on trial. His Honor presided, looking very impressive, flanked by two flags—the American flag and that of California. The tops of the flags were adorned with eagles. The mild face of a deceased judge looked down from the wall, and a dairy advertisement, with a big-letter calendar, hung beside it.

His Honor sat behind a high desk, the bailiff sat lower at his right side, and a poor-looking man was crouched in the witness seat. He maintained he didn't make more than eighteen dollars a week, and that he couldn't pay alimony to his wife. He was a chicken broker. He bought chickens and sold them and that got this tremendous income every week. I looked at the old bitch who demanded ten bucks a week from him. She wasn't worth the money; the man was quite right not to give her a dime. If I were the judge, I'd take just one look at the lady and have the case dismissed without going into details. But no, justice had to take its course. Several witnesses took the stand. Because the man didn't make more than eighteen a week, even the witnesses couldn't force him to pay ten. A young, highly pregnant woman was prepared to give a dramatic performance, but to her disappointment she was asked only one question and sent back to the benches. I felt sorry for her. She was quite good-looking, and I was just going to ask her about her husband when I remembered that *la recherche de la paternitée est interdite*.

I sat and listened, trying to straighten out my own mind. I had to see the judge. Whom else could I see? I didn't trust the police with my secret. The judge was the man to take matters in hand.

I wasn't sure if Joe knew about the whole case. Marshall did, Marjorie Dean did, and Roger Niven did, too, but couldn't do anything about it. Niven had left town after the verdict. Poor Roger Niven, cheated by a bitch!

Well, there was a thunderstorm brewing for Marshall and that woman. The papers would get hold of it, and would throw me right into the spotlight. I might become famous—who knows? They were certainly going to pay me for my story. I'd ask the judge for his advice; what he thought best.

The time passed slowly. "Overruled," the judge said from time to time. "Sustained." "The next witness." The chicken merchant got off, and another case, alimony again, came up.

I began to see my duty very clearly. I was an accessory after the fact, a man who knew about a crime, and it was up to me to inform the court about it. I might get pinched myself, if I didn't. Marshall should have known that he couldn't buy me with his lousy three hundred dollars. Did I look like a man who could be bought cheaply? I was really angry with him for misjudging my character so much. They'd played a very dirty trick on Niven. Now they'd have to watch out.

"Session is closed for today," the bailiff said. The lamps in the courtroom had green glass bowls and a little yellow knob on top, which sent a small beam to the ceiling. The crowd of moochers who sat around amused by the spectacle of the unhappiness of their fellow men filed out, to return punctually tomorrow. The judge left his seat and disappeared behind a door inscribed: PLEASE SEE CLERK BEFORE ENTERING.

In France there wouldn't have been any inscription, and in Germany they'd write: *Eintritt Verboten*. They wouldn't even dream of adding the word "please." They have cut it out of the language.

I left the courtroom and waited in the corridor. After a few moments the judge stepped out, with bowler hat and a different coat. I took a step forward and he looked at me. I said: "Your Honor, I have to see you on a very important matter!" He stopped at once and tried to remember my face. But as there was nothing to remember, I expected him to say: "Overruled!" But he didn't say a word; he left it up to me to continue. I know a lot of people who don't reply; they make you talk and you get into a tight spot quickly.

"It's about Roger Niven's case versus Marjorie Dean," I said, and to my surprise an amazing change came over his features. He had a very somber face, with a big square jaw and very blue eyes which seemed to look right through you. He had learned that from the poor human scum that flocked around his mighty seat of wisdom and justice.

His expression seemed to become menacing. He stood silent, pondering, uncertain what to do next. Finally he turned around and said, "Please follow me...."

He took me to one of the conference rooms and closed the door behind us. He didn't take off his hat, while I, being polite and not feeling so comfortable anymore, turned mine in my hands.

"What's the matter?" he asked gruffly. Well, that was not the tone to use to a man who fought for justice.

"Niven's case was a frame-up and I can prove it. I thought Your Honor would be the best man to talk to before the truth leaks out."

"Who are you?" he said, his hat still on his square head. That was not the right reply to such an important announcement. I felt I should be treated differently. He ought to be only too happy that I did him the honor of informing him first. If I had told the papers first, where would he have been?

"I'm the man who produced the evidence upon which

Your Honor has built the verdict." That got him. He put his hat on a hook and sat down, pointing at a chair. I still disliked his face; it was very unfriendly, threatening. But he couldn't bully me. I hadn't done a thing. I produced the evidence from my pocket, and the *Times* from the week before. While I spread it out on the table, he watched me like a man watching a snake. But I didn't care. Soon he would be crawling on his knees.

"This is the conversation Niven was said to have had with his wife, Marjorie Dean. It was supposedly produced on a Dictaphone record, with the help of a microphone hidden in Niven's room. That's all baloney." I waited. I didn't want to shoot my powder off too quickly. But he didn't say a word. Those awful eyes of his made me quite nervous.

"It's his voice all right, and Miss Dean's, too . . . but although the voice was his, he wasn't speaking to her. That's funny, isn't it? It was his voice but not his sentences. He swore he hadn't said those things to her, and he was right. I'd cut the dialogue out, word by word, from films of his, and put them together. You can do things like that easily with an old sound track. Miss Dean added the missing dialogue lines later; then the whole concoction was transcribed onto the wax disc Your Honor heard in the courtroom. You have been tricked by an artificially produced conversation and some clever lines Miss Dean added! It was foolproof evidence any judge would base his verdict on. Niven recognized his own voice. So what could he do? It was a clever trick, I would even go so far as to call it devilish!"

My God, what a speech! If His Honor wasn't shaken now, I'd never be able to change his stonelike mind.

He looked at me. He obviously was trying to digest what I had told him. Of course, it was very technical; and he didn't know anything about film cutting or sound tracks. He was just trying to understand.

"What's your name?"

"Pierre Bernet."

"You're French?"

"Yes."

"And what are you doing here in our country?"

What a question! I didn't like it. I was a man trying to make a living, like millions of others who came from immigrant stock. What an insult! Besides, it had nothing to do with the Niven case. It was the typical question of an Englishman in England. They just throw out foreigners any time they want. All they do is phone the Home Office and say, "Is that the Home Office? I say, there's a Mr. Bernet. Pierre Bernet, a Frenchman. I owe him a few pounds. It's a disgrace that good English money should be squandered on a foreigner. Please throw him out by tomorrow morning." And sure enough, you can bet on it that early in the morning two gentlemen in bowler hats appear at your door, asking you politely which of the two ports you choose to sail from for the continent, Folkstone or Dover....

But this is the Land of the Free. I had my quota number and was determined to become a full-fledged American. It was impudent of the judge to ask me what I was doing here!

"Sir," I said, "I don't know what your question has to do with the service I'm rendering in the Niven case. I'm fighting for justice. If I hadn't come here, a great injustice would have been committed."

Well, it would do him good to hear about his duties.

"My impression is that you're a very suspicious character," the judge said slowly, still staring at me with his awful eyes. "What is your occupation?"

"Film cutter, sir," I said, and didn't know why I didn't have the strength to get up and walk away.

"And you cut out dialogue from old films, if I follow your accusation rightly?"

"Yes, sir."

"Who paid you?"

"Mr. Marshall."

"I have never heard of him," the judge said. "Did Miss Dean know about it?"

"Certainly! Or she wouldn't have spoken the additional lines." Was he trying to fool me? I suddenly had a terrible premonition that the man who was sitting opposite me knew more about the case than I ever would.

I felt my spine getting cold, the blood running out of my veins.

"How much were you paid for the job?" He had raised his voice a little, and I had the feeling that hundreds of people were listening to our conversation from the next room.

"Three hundred dollars, sir," I said, rather subdued. I couldn't help myself.

"Three hundred dollars! And how long did you work for that money?"

"Four days," I stammered. Everything suddenly looked very much against me, and he got the idea at once.

"Four days . . . I'm not familiar with the salary of a film cutter; I don't know anything about the fantastic incomes of the film people. Please tell me how much your usual salary is when you're working for a film company."

"Well, I got seventy-five dollars a week from M-G-M."

It was absurd; this cross-examination put me in the wrong. Who was the accused? I or Marshall? What was this man up to?

"You got four weeks' salary for four days' work. Don't you think, Mr. Bernet, that it looks very strange for you to complain to me about an injustice, when you, a grown-up intelligent man, must have known that you were doing something wrong? It must have aroused your suspicions that you were paid a sum of money out of proportion to the service you rendered. It was your duty to refuse the job, knowing that something unlawful must be attached to it."

He had me. I felt like an accomplice in the Niven case.

"Your Honor," I said, "there are too many crazy people in this town. I never question what they do. They may pay a thousand dollars for a handshake, and for a lifetime's work a penny. In a business where a man gets a thousand a week, and others pity him for being underpaid, a poor man like me doesn't kick if he is overpaid. I didn't kick. I took the money."

I suddenly found myself in a position where I had to explain. But I was here to accuse, not to defend.

"Can you prove that Miss Dean deliberately spoke the incriminating dialogue in order to get an annulment of her marriage? How do you know that Mr. Niven and Miss Dean didn't engage in the conversation which led to the divorce decree? How can you prove that the work you did was not done for some other reason than to deceive the court of justice?"

"What other reason could there be?" It appeared to

me that he used too many technical terms. He seemed to know something about film cutting, too. His questions were too pat.

"It's not up to me to explain," the judge said, "but may I warn you, Mr. Bernet, you're only a foreigner in a country which you don't know very well. If I were you, I should stick to the work I was doing and not go around accusing important people, at the same time ridiculing the Court of Justice. I'm going to follow up your accusations. But it seems very improbable to me that your story has any foundation whatsoever. It will have repercussions on you if you're not able to prove your insinuations. I'm sorry to have to reprove you. But I've found that people who are guests in a foreign country often do not behave as guests should. Very soon we will have much more stringent immigration laws, to enable us to keep out undesirable elements. Good day."

He snatched up his bowler hat and left hurriedly. I didn't know what to make of the whole situation. He certainly had been very inconsistent in his accusations.

I felt very low and quite suddenly I trembled as if I had fever. I was mixed up in something which had many more consequences than I had divined when I had gone up to see the judge. I was really frightened and couldn't make out why.

When I'm in a spot, I usually sit down and trace the fear back to its source. I sat down now and considered the whole case, trying to find the exact point where fear had entered the scene. There was no reason for fear. I was right, and they had to be damned careful if they wanted to do anything to me. Here the fear had started! That was it! They could do things against me!

But what? Take away the job I didn't have?

I spat to the side of the spittoon purposely to soil the town hall, and went down in the Tower express. It was rather late in the day. The uniformed rattler had already left. I was nearly alone. For some reason, not clear to me, I disliked leaving the building. I listened while a gentleman explained to me a miniature landscape with rivers and power stations, pointing with a long stick to several spots, telling me something about the future development of the power and water of the town of Los Angeles. They had only water enough for eight million people, and now they were worried and something had to be done at once for the future. One had to be prepared for the day when the population of Los Angeles would exceed that number, and all signs indicated that Los Angeles was going to be the greatest and biggest city in the world.

I listened to him attentively without knowing exactly what he was worrying about. He finally bade me good night and walked away with his long stick. I left the city hall slowly, and saw in the entrance for the first time those two faces which I will never forget.

One of the men had cauliflower ears, a nose which pointed toward his left shoulder, and a face which should have made him permanently discontented with life. He was such an obvious type that he couldn't hide on the bottom of the Pacific Ocean without being discovered at once. The other was a thin fellow with reddish hair and a lipless mouth. He had glasses on his stubby nose. They were standing in the doorway when I passed, and they spoke to each other.

I went to the parking lot and paid two bits.

The town was crowded with traffic. It was dark by now, the rush hour when everyone wants to get home quickly.

Here the night comes down like a curtain, in a matter of seconds, to prove that California has a subtropical climate.

I picked up a poor chap who was waiting for the bus and gave him a lift to Western Avenue. Then I again looked for somebody to take along because I dreaded driving alone. Slowing down, I had just wheeled into one of the side streets when my car was smashed from behind by an Oldsmobile. My head was jerked forward, and I hit my nose on the steering wheel. I stopped and looked behind me. I was pushed again and again. I drove to the curb. The car behind me stopped and two men stepped out.

"What the hell were you shouting at us?" the crooked-nosed one barked. "What d'ya think you are?"

He didn't give me a chance to defend myself, but hit me on the jaw and I went numb. Of course, I tried to hit back. This was no time to exchange explanations. He talked incessantly while he hit me again and again.

"We'll teach you to keep your mouth shut, you bastard. You do what you're told and nothing else. You'd be better off in a wooden kimono. Whaddya think you're paid for—to squeal? The next time you'll get a bullet!"

I fell down and faintly heard a crash. My whole body burned intensely. I couldn't see anything anymore—blood was running down my face, and my right hand where I hit the man was numb. He had used a blackjack, I was sure.

I don't know how long it was before I could think again. When I opened my eyes, a woman was bending over me, pouring some water between my clenched teeth. I couldn't swallow, and spat it out. Somebody was wiping the blood off my face. I staggered to my feet and looked around.

"Your car is all smashed up," the woman said comfortingly. She talked slowly, syllable by syllable, to make me understand. "I've called an ambulance. They should be here any minute . . ."

There stood my car, its side bashed in. No use repairing it; the whole car wasn't worth much more than a hundred bucks in running order. Now it was nothing but junk. The thugs had left. The whole thing couldn't have lasted longer than one minute.

People walked by. Nobody seemed to be curious. They had seen people with bloody faces and smashed-up cars too often.

"These dangerous crossroads . . ." the woman said soothingly.

I felt every tooth in my mouth wobble. My arm was hurting.

There was a siren and an ambulance, and suddenly the place became a center of interest.

"Where's the corpse?" a voice called. A man in white jumped off the back step. Somebody else opened the double door.

Intense fear nearly drowned my consciousness. My mind was still paralyzed, but the fear was there and directed my actions.

"Did you break something?" The attendant of the ambulance seemed to be somewhat disappointed, but still he kept his hopeful air.

There was the Law, too, in khaki, on a motorcycle. The Law was interested in my wrecked car.

"I'll call a garage. I know a very cheap place to have your bus repaired," he said persuasively.

"I'm not insured," I managed to mumble, "and I have

no money, either."

"Oh," he said. He was disappointed too. I wasn't good business for either the ambulance or the police. The policeman would have called the garage to get his cut on the repair bill, and the ambulance would have entered me in a hospital. I was very poor business indeed.

"I'll have your car towed away," the policeman said, determined, and without waiting for a reply, he took off noisily.

"I can take you to a good doctor who'll dress your cuts," the man from the ambulance said, losing hope. I didn't look too prosperous to him, so he was careful to add, "It won't cost you more than a couple of bucks to get fixed up."

I shook my head, unable to talk.

"Who called us, anyhow?" the man in white cried, directing his bad humor at all the onlookers. They began to move. Nobody wanted to be responsible. The woman who had called the ambulance had left, too.

"Forget it, Fred!" the driver of the hospital car called from his seat. "Let's go—they need us more somewhere else."

The man in white stepped inside the ambulance, and they left as noisily as the cop on his motorbike. They feel very important when they can keep their sirens going full blast.

Nobody had bothered to ask me about the accident. It was no accident; it was something close to murder. But it was not interesting enough for them because it was poor business—no ambulance, no repairs, nothing but a wrecked car to tow away. A greenback for the cop, that's all it amounted to.

The blood had stopped and a taxi was already

waiting. They're always present when they smell business.

"Taxi, sir?" the man in the yellow cab called cheerfully. "I'll take you home. They'll haul your car away—but your name and address is in it, I s'pose . . ."

He politely held open the door, looking at me inquisitively to see if I were going to soil his clean upholstery.

9

I was considerate enough to enter my apartment house by the side door. I didn't want to make a spectacle of myself, but Miss Bowden at the desk saw me. Her face lost all its color and her nostrils looked pinched. Even in my terrible state, I had to laugh.

That upset her so completely she couldn't open her mouth. I passed her as quickly as I could in my present condition.

I crawled upstairs without taking the elevator, locked the door behind me, and looked in the mirror.

Miss Bowden had had herself well in hand not to faint when she saw me. I looked like the colored cover of a *True Detective Magazine*. My forehead was splashed with dry blood, my eyes were almost shut, my mouth was twisted down at one corner. My jaw was swollen on the side where the blackjack had hit it.

I stuck my head under the cold shower and didn't give a damn if the water ruined my suit. Liquid fire flowed over my face. My skin began to burn. The air was suddenly punctuated with dots of flame and a tremendous roaring noise seemed to fill the room.

I was going to faint.

I clenched my teeth until this fantastic sensation faded. The water felt cool and soothing now.

I got rid of my wet clothes and began to think hard, with my head still under the shower.

I had to talk to someone. Eleanor!

Eleanor, who was born and brought up here, would be able to explain all this. Like all the kids I had met, she had a very healthy, direct, unsentimental approach to life. She would throw some light on the mystery.

I turned the water off. My skin was beginning to hurt again, but that was a simple punishment and I suffered it as a sort of purifying process. In fact, I wanted it to hurt more. And, as I wished the pain would grow stronger, it almost ceased.

Lying on the bed, I tried to straighten out my thoughts. Eleanor must be told. I picked up the phone. Her mother answered. Eleanor was working, but she would be through at six and come right up to see me. Mother would take care of that.

I fell into a doze. My skin began to burn again and every bone in my body shouted its existence.

There was a knock at the door. Miss Bowden's voice called me, and I managed to tell her not to disturb me. She went away, happy that I was still alive.

Dying must be something like what I felt . . . slipping away into a soothing black void, without further wish or ambition, without restraint or resistance.

When I woke I heard Eleanor knocking.

I unlocked the door. She looked very beautiful in full war regalia, still wearing her false eyelashes and studio make-up. She could not turn pale under the grease paint, but her eyes opened wide.

"For heaven's sake!" she gasped.

I smiled with one corner of my swollen mouth.

"Don't be frightened," I said. "I'm still alive."

I went back and lay down and closed my eyes. She took my hand. She was a very sensible girl—she didn't ask a thing.

Minutes went by. I felt happy. Why couldn't I keep her like this forever? She gave me so much strength and comfort. I would find work. I would be a success. I would live, if she would just give me a chance . . .

"I went down to City Hall today," I said, "and when I came out, two toughs beat me up. It's all very mysterious to me. Perhaps you can tell me why it happened. I haven't done anything wrong."

"Why don't you tell the police?" she asked.

"Because they would kill me."

"The police?"

She was astonished and frightened. She sensed some mystery here that made her tremble. She wasn't a coward, but she didn't know me very well. I might be a murderer for all she knew.

"No—Marshall's gangsters!"

Now it was out. She didn't answer.

"The job Joe gave me to do was something illegal. I tried to tell the judge. Those men came after me and beat me up."

That was information enough for her.

"You're a fool," she said. I heard the deep note that came into her voice only when she was very angry.

"If Marshall's mixed up in something crooked, you can't just go to a judge and tell him! If Marshall gave you a dirty job to do, he knew how to protect himself. He wouldn't let *you* get him into trouble."

Resolutely, she went into the dressing room and took the telephone with her. I didn't try to listen to her voice. It seemed to be speaking very far away. I closed my eyes. She was taking care of me. I felt safe and content.

She returned quickly.

"I've phoned Joe. He'll be over soon."

I didn't open my eyes. I was sick with disgust. Was she using my misfortune just to see Joe? As a welcome excuse? I had to get beaten up to give her a chance to be in the same room with her lover!

She sat down and put her hand on my forehead. It was light and cool. I felt her lips on my cheek, breathing close to me for a little while. She was pitying me. She realized that Joe was responsible for this, but she didn't know what to make of the whole situation.

"Joe will tell you what to do," she whispered.

I could have cried. What did I want Joe for? He would take her away from me as soon as he walked into the room.

It was just as I expected. He came in without knocking—a lithe, slightly stooped saint. He didn't look at me; he looked at Eleanor. He smiled at her. There he stood, taking possession of her by his mere presence.

"Hello, Joe," she said.

That was not her voice. She had never used that tone with me.

"What happened to Pierre?" he asked.

His voice was dry, very matter-of-fact. He didn't even shake hands with Eleanor. He came right over to my bed and sat down.

I looked up into his face. It was not the face I knew. It didn't look soft and insipid any more. His eyes were strong. They shone with a clear blue light.

"Marshall's men beat me up," I said and sat up.

"Why?" he asked. And before I realized that I had wanted him to explain, I answered him.

"I went to the judge who gave Marjorie Dean her divorce. And when I came out two men followed me."

"You're a fool, Pierre!"

I realized that he had called me by my first name. It was a shock, but not an unpleasant one.

"I advised you to do your job and not to bother about anything else. It wasn't your business to meddle with things that didn't concern you. Miss Dean got her divorce. That's what Marshall wanted. I didn't know what his plans for her were, but he certainly had to protect her against any foolish steps you might take. He's a friend of the judge. How could you be so stupid!"

He didn't raise his voice while he talked. He looked into my eyes, and that other side of his nature showed itself again—in a pleading expression that begged for understanding.

He bent his head, and nobody spoke for a while.

Eleanor looked at him. One of her eyelashes had fallen off. The right side of her face was that of a stilted angel, too beautiful to be real. The other was human, childlike, tender.

There was no doubt that she loved Joe to an extent I couldn't even guess. It was beyond my comprehension. I lack even the ability to imagine myself in a state of mind like hers. I'm always conscious, critical—my damned brain never gives me a rest. It's always thinking and I can't switch it off for a moment. Even when I suffer, I suffer with my brain and not with my heart.

Joe seemed to think with his heart. He was listening to a voice only he could hear, which told him what to do. How convenient! If I had a voice like that, it would have told me not to talk to the judge.

"You're mistaken," Joe said in a low kind voice. "It's not in my power to do anything. I can't help you. Except with advice. And advice is the cheapest kind of help—but sometimes it's important. Please don't misunderstand me. I didn't know what Marshall was up to when he rented my cutting room. It wasn't my business to ask him.

"But I do know that Marjorie Dean is a very unhappy woman. She was tied to a man she didn't love. And she has nothing to hold to, no belief, no hope—and, in spite of the gay life she lives, no joy. She wanted to part with that man Niven, but he wouldn't give her her freedom.

"Marshall helped her. You helped her, too, without knowing how valuable your assistance was to her. She got her divorce.

"The way she got it seems cruel. But it was an operation. Operations are never painless. If people aren't careful not to become ill, they have to suffer. That's how it was. She was ill and Niven wouldn't see it. She is a beautiful woman, and young!

"And then—you came along.

"Marshall had to take his precautions. He sent his men after you. He doesn't know any other way. I'm sorry for you, Pierre—but why didn't you stay out of it? Would it make you happy if Miss Dean had to go back into the cage she hated so much?

"When you have a complaint, you should go to the people who've done you harm. You believe Miss Dean has harmed you. Why don't you go to her? Or to Marshall? Do you know so much about her that you dare judge her? Hear her defense first, before you condemn her! I'm sorry, Pierre—that I have to talk to you like this."

Of course, he had to defend Marjorie Dean. He was defending himself! He was in a cage with someone he hated, too—and trying to get away! Defending her, he was pleading his own case. I should have thought of that!

But what was he hinting? Was I to see Marjorie Dean? He had put it very clearly. Maybe it was a good idea. I had nothing to lose. I wouldn't be slugged for talking to the lady.

I couldn't get a clear idea in my head anyway. It hurt when I tried to think. Somehow, Marshall and the judge had cooked up the whole business, and like a fool, I had run right into the barbed wire. I was lucky they hadn't finished me off. I ought to be thankful that I was still alive. Joe had hinted at that in his careful, pretty speech.

"Thank you, Joe," I murmured.

He put his thin white hand in mine.

"Forgive me, Pierre," he said again, and smiled. It was a kind smile. He could express more with his eyes and his smile than with all his perfectly chosen words.

I felt his strange fascination. I knew he was constantly throwing himself away for other people, reducing his ego to zero. That was what made him so acceptable at times. He didn't use his power consciously —I couldn't accuse him of that.

He was much stronger than I have ever been. He knew where he was going. Perhaps he could help me, too.

"Now I must leave."

He got up and took Eleanor in his arms. He held her close, without sensual desire.

She belonged to him. Nothing that needed explaining

stood between them.

"Good-bye, Eleanor—we will be together soon."

He paused at the door to smile back at me.

10

Eight days in my room! My chin still hurt. I had enough time to think, lying on my bed for hours at a stretch, while the sun traced the little flowers of the curtain on my floor. For hours and hours I lay there, straightening out things, making plans, trying to find myself.

Little Emily came up three times, looking neat and healthy. She chatted along, talked about her work, cast a very kind eye on me. Like a good comrade, she cheered me up. And she didn't inquire about my swollen chin. She brought me cigarettes, found out what I liked to eat, and unpacked a small fried chicken which you get on Hollywood Boulevard for sixty cents.

One afternoon she ran out of conversation and we sat in silence until the sun began to sink and Eleanor came in.

She, too, had some parcels in her hand. She saw Emily and smiled at her, put the parcels down, then went into the kitchen and prepared a meal in no time. There were even a couple of bottles of beer among the things she had brought. We all ate and a friendly spirit grew up among us. I avoided any serious talk. I had fallen in love with Eleanor all over again, but seeing her so matter of fact, I closed up like an oyster. It was like the moment before an earthquake starts. Nature held its breath, tension was in the air, and an explosion had to come sooner or later. Eleanor felt it;

Emily did, too. Nothing was said about Marjorie Dean. Everything was up to me now. I had convinced myself that I must follow Joe's advice and see Miss Dean. This idea became a kind of obsession; it seemed to be the only solution to all this trouble.

Next afternoon I walked down Hollywood Boulevard. I felt like a man who had been confined in a hospital for weeks. I hadn't eaten very much in those days, and my body had shed the poisons which accumulate with food. I felt clean and transparent and light. My mind was floating in crystal. I moved carefully lest that precious brain of mine break. I saw my future life before me, rather distinguished, and I knew with certainty it would end soon—break like a thread in a weaving machine, leaving behind a loom of unfinished material. But this conviction did not frighten me; it was natural and inevitable; a perfect end for an imperfect life.

Walking along, I looked into the faces of girls, but none of them even glanced back. They don't do it here in Hollywood. They wear an expression of disgust and offense, as if a look into their eyes were molestation. They behave differently from any girls in any other town in the world. How friendly they are in San Francisco! They even smile at you, and you carry their smile as a gift with you to the next face. And this strange, unfriendly attitude of the people in the "Town of Two Dimensions" is one reason for the unhappiness of all of them. They consider their fellow man an enemy until he proves himself a friend, instead of calling him a friend until he turns out to be an enemy. They don't count from plus to minus—they count from minus to plus! This makes them all seem miserable.

I looked at my face in a window. My cheeks were

pale, my eyes big, my lips nearly bloodless. My expression was ethereal. The blue spots had gone; the chin had shrunken back to its normal size.

I was in shape to be seen by Marjorie Dean.

She lived at Beford Drive in Beverly Hills. I walked down the Boulevard, crossed over to Sunset. I took my time. She might not be home; she might not even receive me. I wasn't sure what I wanted to say to her. The foggy course of my destiny went in that direction. I had to go to her.

The house was not very impressive. It showed a broad lawn in front, without flowers. The grass was green and well-kept. The house was built in Spanish style like most of the houses, with big windows and dark wooden frames. When I rang, a dog barked faintly in a high voice. A Negro opened. He was a husky fellow in a white coat, trained to chase away autograph hunters and salesmen.

"I want to see Miss Dean," I said politely and determinedly. It didn't enter my mind that he might send me away. That determination obviously impressed him. "Mr. Marshall sent me," I concluded.

That seemed to be the password, because he bowed and let me in. "One moment, sir," he said, and dissolved.

I looked around. She surely was a girl with taste. The huge hall, with an enormous flower vase, had a precious carpet on the floor, white walls, very bare, and old doors with heavy carvings, obviously taken from a mission. There was nothing to destroy or disturb the balance of doors and walls, ceiling and floor. She was no snob—or she had an architect in whom she believed implicitly.

The black man took shape again near me and asked

me to follow him into a room which had red walls. The doors opened into a wide garden where a blue swimming pool, flanked by trees, reflected the sinking sun. The furniture of this room was heavy; enormous pieces stood about. I felt lost and small.

For a moment I considered running away through the garden toward the wall I couldn't see.

When I turned around, she was standing in the doorway. She had been watching me for a minute or so. She got that trick from Marshall. She was his pupil. He was Svengali; Trilby stood here. And she looked like Trilby. She was the first film star I ever saw who was more beautiful in life than on the screen. That was because most film stars are not beautiful, but are very plain. Nobody would see anything extraordinary in them if the camera did not bring it out. But this girl's coloring was startling: red hair, white skin, green eyes. She was not very tall, but she was stunning. God had overdone her; had given her too much. I had thought only the artists of *Cosmopolitan* could create faces like hers.

We looked at each other a minute. She was a tigress with a red wig. She wore a dress of a yellowish color— the first red-haired girl I'd ever seen who did not wear green. That got me; I had to laugh. Her face changed and she seemed to be annoyed.

"Pardon my hilarity," I said, "but you're the first redhead I ever met who didn't wear green . . ."

"I dislike green," she said. Her voice was full of charm, high and deliberate.

"It would be too much color on you, anyhow," I said toward the door where she stood. "You should be kind to human beings and keep them from overstraining their eyes."

Now she had to laugh, too. The expression of her eyes changed. She had obviously made up her mind. She was independent enough to know at once what she wanted.

"Sit down," she said, and walked toward me. She knew how to walk. "Mr. Marshall sent you?" She was sitting opposite me in a deep chair which towered over her frail white face.

"No," I admitted. She did not seem to be astonished.

"Lonza let you in," she said, believing in the colored man's infallible judgment.

"Ali Baba knew the word 'Sesame' which would open the mountain . . . I knew the password for your house . . ."

"And what do you want?" She was impressed. She did not show it, but I felt that I might have some influence over her. I never would have expected it.

"To see you," I said simply.

She looked at me. She did not move her dark eyelashes. I held her gaze. I couldn't give up now without losing out forever.

"It is dangerous to be a fool," she said.

"I have nothing to lose."

"You are a fool," she said with her soft and silvery voice.

"What of it?" I smiled. "If it's dangerous to be a fool, then I always have been a fool. I don't care what happens to me tomorrow. I only care what happens to me at this moment. I am not conceited enough to live for the future. You can't take care of it. My father tried to take care of his. He saved all his money for a big funeral. Then he fell into a blast furnace, and never got a funeral at all. That made me think."

She laughed loudly. Her face suddenly became

vulgar. Her laughter betrayed her upbringing.

"Who are you?" she asked suddenly, very sober.

"I helped you to get rid of your husband," I said.

Her face changed. She no longer looked approachable. Her green eyes became very dark.

"What do you know about it?"

"Not very much—I'm only the poor film cutter who built the incriminating dialogue which gave you your freedom. I tried to talk to the judge, but he wouldn't even listen. I got beaten up by people who were hired by a man I think you know. All that was very unpleasant and dangerous. And now I am here to see you. I had to see you; my sense of justice made me. It may cost me my health—but I'm assuming you're not as violent and brutal as the man who had me beaten up."

Her hand moved. I saw the bell on the little table next to her. I would be lost as soon as she should ring. I had no chance against Lonza.

I said, quickly: "Everyone shoots first, and asks questions afterwards. Nobody ever plays ball. They have no time for that any more. Well—I think I'll be off—"

Her hand stopped; her eyes became curious.

"What do you want?" she asked, leaning back. She took my measure, like a man looking at a girl, beginning with the hair and finishing up with the shoes. When girls look at girls, they begin with the shoes and end up with the face.

I sat down again, feeling I weighed two tons. Since was opening a new business and entering the guild of blackmailers, I wanted to say: "Money." But I couldn't say it. I just smiled sheepishly.

She waited. She didn't help me. I lit a cigarette I

took from a little silver box on the table, and inhaled the smoke deeply. But even that moment ended and I still didn't know what to say.

She finished sizing me up, and rose.

"Well?" There was no mystery anymore; she knew why I had come. The words stopped in my throat and choked me. I couldn't get them out. I was a very poor blackmailer.

I managed to shrug my shoulders nonchalantly. "Besides, I wanted to meet you—like other people enjoy collecting stamps, I like to talk to beautiful women . . ."

What nonsense! She still smiled, but the expression of amusement had changed. She pitied me.

"You're not very good at your profession! I've met much better blackmailers. You've no technique whatever!" She laughed. I certainly amused her. Her teeth were very even; her mouth big and red. She was a beautiful piece of flesh. All right—if she knew so much, she could stand a little more.

"You're right. It's my first. It's a shame I bungled it, but one must begin somehow. Why do they always ask for good references here in this town? Even if I'm a rotten blackmailer now, maybe I'll improve later. Just give me a chance."

"I'm not going to encourage you . . . You won't get a penny out of me . . ." She came closer, her tiny bare feet were very white, with red nails and long thin toes.

"I didn't ask you for anything," I said, and got up. "I'm a fool . . . Please don't make me feel bad because I'm a fool! May I go now?"

"I'll take you to the door," she said, and walked in front of me, carrying her red hair like a torch.

We crossed the big hall and she opened the door for me.

"Against the big competitors, I've no chance. Sorry that I'm such a poor crook," I said.

She looked at me with her green eyes, but I couldn't fathom her thoughts. "What's your name?" she asked.

"Pierre Bernet," I said, intrigued by her kind interest in my person.

"Do you have a tuxedo?"

"I even have tails—from Davies in London," I joked, but it sounded hollow.

"Put on your tails and call for me at eight . . ."

"I've no car—but I live at Cherokee and Yucca . . ."

"I'll be there at ten past eight. Can you drive?"

"The right question to ask a foreigner."

"A tout à l'heure, Pierre!" she said, without any accent.

"A tout à l'heure, Marjorie."

The door closed behind me. I marched down Beverly Hills. Some people seem to like fools at that. But she didn't interest me in the least.

11

At ten minutes past eight, a Cadillac 75 coupé stopped at the sign near the hibiscus tree. It stood there and waited for me. I could see the long red hood from my window.

With a last quick look into the mirror on the bathroom door, I left. I had lost weight. The smartly cut tailcoat floated loose from my thin body, revealing the masterly elegance of its historic splendor. It was of dark blue silk, cut unobtrusively, as only English tailors, with prewar training and a haughty feeling for understatement, could do it.

But Marjorie noticed it at once; a smile and a small gleam in her eyes betrayed her.

"Behold! A real gentleman!" she exclaimed mockingly, and moved from the driver's seat over to the other door. "Is it cricket, sir, to let a fair lady wait?"

"The fair lady doesn't ride a steed, but drives a 1941 automobile," I said and stepped into the car. "She should say: 'Hey, damn it, shake a leg'!"

She laughed and pulled down the rearview mirror to study her face. I started the car and moved off. "Where to?" I asked.

"Club Femina," she said, and took a lipstick out of the dashboard compartment. She went to work at painting her lips, absorbed, thoughtful, forgetting about me as completely as if I were her liveried chauffeur.

"I need further instructions, Madame," I said, smartly. The car moved noiselessly, smoothly.

"What do you mean?" she drawled.

"Well . . . just stop and think a moment. Use that well-rested mind. Or are you only used to stooges?" I turned and put my hand under her chin. She pulled away at once. She disliked any intimacy she had not indicated.

I was tempted to stop the car, leave the wheel and walk home. She sensed my reaction—it may be that I had already slowed down—and said quickly:

"I'm taking you out to dinner. Didn't I tell you?"

"You did not," I stated and stepped on the gas. "I'm in a strange mood tonight. I want to talk to a human being—just for a change. A human being distinguishes itself from animals by social perceptions, which consider the other person's moods and feelings and act accordingly. Animals don't have those perceptions. Now be considerate—if only for the sake of novelty. You've asked me out tonight—a bold gesture of feminine independence. I might say a dangerous gesture. Tell me what you have in mind. I may have no money, but I'm not a gigolo, either. I might have a fit of pride and step out of this three-thousand-dollar bus and leave you to drive up to that expensive club alone. Money is the cheapest form of aristocracy. It only arouses my contempt."

"You're nuts," she said, putting the lipstick away and moving closer to me. "People wear slacks in this town—no tails and white ties—even on their minds."

"Do you like that?" I asked.

"No," she replied in a girlish voice. The red leather seat was wide enough for three people. Sitting in the middle of it, she was still far away from me.

I had ten dollars in my pocket, and I wondered how the adventure would develop. Would she pay for dinner with a bill casually slipped under the check? Or would she discreetly put some money into my pocket, or pass it to me under the table?

I had never before been taken out by a woman, and I felt at a loss. Maybe I should gamble with my ten bucks, throwing it on red at the roulette table—double or nothing. Maybe twenty dollars was enough to pay for dinner and drinks in such a tony place. Wouldn't it surprise her if I paid . . . a thought which would never have entered Jerry's mind. I took pleasure in lingering on the idea of buying dinner for a lady who earned as much in one day as I had the whole year past.

"What are you thinking of?" She turned her clear

gaze on me and tried to read my thoughts. She was very conscious of her beauty, sure of the impression she made on men. But in my case she was mistaken. And strangely enough she seemed to sense it. Her eyes began to flutter.

To me she was like a reflection in a mirror—something bodiless, unreal, two-dimensional. She was a perfect creation of this town: a hothouse orchid, artificially conceived, living an artificial life, created for an artificial undertaking. She had to be photographed to be concrete.

"What's the matter?" she asked uneasily. Then, as I did not reply, she shrugged her shoulders in the soft mink coat and opened her powder box.

We drove up to the club and left the car with an attendant. A bouncer behind a wrought-iron gate opened quickly when he saw her coming.

I hadn't been to this place before and was slightly disappointed. It was like a cheap movie set, built to be broken up after two days' shooting. Clubs are built and opened on the run in this town, and it seems not to pay to spend money for anything more durable than plaster.

Stark white walls; indirect lighting; a few chairs and couches scattered about; artificial flowers in huge vases.

The hat-check girl looked at Marjorie with melting eyes and Marjorie smiled knowingly in her direction. The girl blushed. But, as I had no hat and Marjorie's mink coat was too beautiful not to be seen in the dining room, she didn't come forward.

Two very young and pretty girls loitered about in shorts and artistically ragged blouses, with extremely long stockings on their long legs. It is the custom of clubs here to sell cigarettes with striptease.

Marjorie waited leisurely in the middle of the lounge to be seen by everybody. I kept in the background, but the eyes of the guests were focused on me. A fat woman, sailing along like a galleon complete with pennants, arrived in a favoring gust of wind and anchored close to us. She greeted Marjorie with a heavy broadside of compliments, but her round curious eyes stared at me. Marjorie ignored her curiosity. Fortunately, the head waiter, his face portraying polite agony, appeared and put an end to this sadistic scene. Marjorie waved the galleon away and took my arm casually.

"Tomorrow you'll be in Miss Francis' column . . . she won't sleep all night for not having found out who you are!"

"But if she does find out—will it damage your social standing?" I pulled her closer to me while we were walking behind the waiter. I could smell the scent of her powder.

"I don't know—yet," she said quietly, and halted. Involuntarily I stepped back. She moved on, a few inches ahead of me.

"Madame," the waiter said with a heavy Italian accent, "I am desolate—I didn't have any reservation from you—why didn't you tell your secretary to phone me?" He wrung his hands in despair. "But I'll find a table for you at once . . . it will be only minutes. Please be patient—do you care to have a drink in the meantime? I really am desolate!"

Marjorie had waited patiently until his moaning stopped.

"All right, Carlo, we're not in a hurry . . ." she said. At once the exaggerated despair was wiped from his face, and he hurried away while we entered the bar.

It was a rather smoky, noisy place. Music could be heard sporadically from the adjoining dining room, which was separated from the bar by a wide glass door.

Every seat was occupied. On the high bar stools— screwed to the floor according to an old California law, to make throwing them difficult—and between the stools, a noisy crowd of furred ladies and highly animated gentlemen received their drinks from the bartender.

The most highly paid employees in the world, actors and producers, were standing about—one hundred thousand dollars' worth of weekly pay checks had gathered in a corner—while some five-dollar girls turned their backs on them. Real democracy ruled there. People rubbed elbows with celebrities and didn't look at them—were even annoyed if they didn't get their drinks ahead of the three-hundred-thousand-dollar idol who had ordered at the same time.

Marjorie pushed her way to the bar, using her elbows. And people reluctantly made room for her.

"Sherry," she ordered and turned questioningly to me.

"Pernod," I said.

Was it part of the understanding that, like a man, she invited me to drink with her? I squeezed myself close to her and said, "Please don't bother . . . I'll get them for you . . ."

A bar stool became vacant and Marjorie quickly took possession of it. She seemed to enjoy the scuffle with the other people.

"I love overcrowded bars," she smiled, displaying her even teeth. "In New York, after the show, we always ate in a small cafeteria where we had to fight to get the food quickly. We were all so hungry that one night one of the girls, ravenous, grabbed a waiter instead of a sandwich . . ."

"Looking at your teeth, I would guess that you were the girl," I laughed.

"What's wrong with my teeth?" she asked with feigned astonishment.

"To be honest, Marjorie, I'm getting a little tired of examining you—and finding nothing that is not perfect . . . teeth, hair, eyes, complexion, figure . . ."

"Well . . ." she said, bored. She had heard these compliments too often.

"You're not dangerous . . . only plain girls are dangerous. Men are on the defensive when they're talking to a good-looking girl. They think twice. But a plain girl always catches her man off guard. That couldn't happen to me with you . . ."

"Thanks," she said, slightly vexed. "It seems to be a disadvantage to be good-looking . . ."

"It depends on what you want from life." I pushed the glass of sherry the bartender had shoved toward me to her and drank the Pernod in a hurry. Since I had eaten little the whole day, the drink hit me at once, as I had expected. My first reaction to this green poison is always pleasant. Its smell, the fragrance of anise, the bitter aftertaste, makes me feel happy, clears my clumsy mind. It affects me as opium does a Chinese. All the riddles of the world seem easy to solve. I need only stretch out my hands and there they are, disentangled, solved. It seems no effort to do it. And because it seems so easy, so simple to accomplish, I never bother . . .

"Another Pernod," I ordered, "and a sherry . . ." I put

my ten dollars on the bar.

"Not for me," Marjorie said. Her glass was untouched. "It's not that I'm a teetotaler—I just don't like the taste of alcohol."

I got back seven dollars and fifty cents change, and generously tipped the man a buck. That's what the Pernod did for the bartender.

"Just swimming in money," said a voice behind me. Marjorie looked up and her eyelids fluttered for a moment. Then she smiled, with perfect control of mouth, eyes and tone.

"Hello, Fred!"

It was Marshall.

"You know Pierre Bernet?" She tugged at his sleeve with a gesture of intimacy.

"Hello, Bernet," Marshall said. He fixed his eyes on me. They were frozen, dirty water. He was slightly drunk as usual. "Moving up the social ladder, I see . . ."

"Right! Last time, I was out with you!" I answered sweetly.

"We seem to run into each other often lately," he said. And to make it plain where he stood, he added, "A little too often!"

I downed the second Pernod and heard the alcohol sing in my ears.

"Have a drink with me," I offered. "It's a pleasure to buy you one this time!"

"Okay." He moved over to Marjorie's left side. "You like Marjorie?" he asked over her head, with a cruel leer.

"You certainly like her," I replied. "Can you blame me for feeling as you do?"

Behind Marshall I saw Jerry appear, looking at me reproachfully. I smiled at him, but he shook his head in warning. I remembered that Marshall was touchy about the girls he liked.

Marjorie, too, was irritated. But she tried to smooth the tension.

"Pierre is a nice boy," she said to Marshall, "if you only knew him . . ."

"I'll tell you a story . . ." Marshall turned to her, but intentionally spoke loud enough for the whole bar to hear. "A very sick man went to a doctor to find out what was ailing him. The doctor took just one look at him. 'Man,' he said, 'you have syphilis!' But the patient closed his coat and picked up his hat. 'Don't you understand—you're sick!' the doctor said again. 'How do you know for sure?' the patient replied. 'You represent only one man's opinion!'"

He grinned at me and downed his drink. I saw faces turn toward me. Nobody laughed.

"There's blood on your lips!" I said loudly.

He whipped out his handkerchief, touched his lips and looked at the white linen. It was not soiled at all. His face suddenly looked greenish; his jaw trembled. The effect had been greater than I had foreseen.

Marjorie got up at once and grabbed my arm. "Come on—quickly," she said hoarsely. She walked away and all I could do was follow her. I caught up with her in the dining room, where Carlo was just saying obsequiously: "Madame, I have succeeded in securing you the very best table. Please follow me, *prego!*"

The best table was in a corner near the music. Carlo pulled Marjorie's chair back and helped her to take off her mink coat. She sat down and picked up the menu, perfectly under control.

"Hungry?" she asked, and didn't wait for a reply.

"Bring anything, Carlo," she said. She smiled at him

as if he were the majority stockholder of a picture company. He bowed and dissolved so quickly that I didn't have time to order another Pernod.

We sat silent. I looked around.

The band was excellent. They were aware of the importance of this engagement as a stepping stone to success in pictures. This was the right place to be "discovered."

People danced. I watched them, but I couldn't distinguish their faces. They passed by like shadows. Opposite us, at the other end of the bandstand, a man sitting alone was staring at us. The waiter had just served him, but he seemed unaware of it. He was middle-aged, gray-haired, his lean face lined. I knew his features, as I knew the faces of most of the men and women who filled the room.

He lit a match. His hand trembled and he couldn't find the end of the cigarette with the flame. The light burned out and he was still staring at us. It was embarrassing. He stared at me—not at Marjorie—until I had to turn away, irritated.

"Don't shout at me," I said. "I know I shouldn't have offended Marshall . . . I regret it—not that I said it, but because it was in very low taste."

Marjorie shrugged her shoulders. "Let's forget it. It can't be helped now."

She was nervous and upset, and broke the cigarette in her hand.

"Don't worry about me," I said. "I can take care of myself." And I added jokingly, "I hope!"

But it didn't seem to be a joke to her. She looked up sharply, deadly serious.

Again I had to look toward the man with the gray hair. He was still staring at me. Marjorie followed my gaze.

"It's Niven," she said. "Just disregard him. He'll try to make your acquaintance, I'm sure . . . "

"Why are you so sure? I understand he's in love with *you!*" I was disgusted with my own cheap jokes.

"He wouldn't dare talk to me," she answered dryly. The waiter arrived with the hors d'oeuvres.

"Bring me a Pernod," I ordered, and waited till the man was out of hearing.

"When I think how the studio and the fan magazines play you up as the simple little girl, the Cinderella of the screen . . . and I watch you here among the lunatics . . . pardon my question: why, for heaven's sake, do you find this mortuary amusing?"

She tasted the seafood cocktail, stirred it slowly and deliberately, pushed it back.

"Let's dance," she said and rose. "Don't bother—Carlo will take care of my coat."

I took her in my arms. She was half a head shorter than I. I looked down at her hair in which the lights were reflected as if in polished bronze.

"You have been taught to dance alone, haven't you?" I asked. She looked up in surprise.

"Of course . . . I was a dancer on the stage, you know."

"I didn't know . . . but I can feel it. You dance too . . . independently. You're used to leading your partner. Pardon me, but I like to lead when I'm dancing." And I pulled her closer. She complied and adapted her movements to mine. She seemed to be less serious.

Niven's eyes followed us. He seemed to see us even when the crowd hid us. He was omnipresent. His proximity was embarrassing. I didn't like it.

"Very hungry?" I asked her. She was dancing now without restraint. Relieved of Niven's presence, I'd have liked to go on for a long time.

"Not a bit . . . I'd only eat dinner to be polite . . ." she said.

"I take the intention for the deed . . ."

She stopped at once and took my arm. "Then come on . . . What are we waiting for?"

We walked down a corridor, where bouncers in evening clothes, casual and silent, leaned against the walls, watching the passers-by. We entered the sanctum—the gambling rooms.

Immediately the atmosphere was different. It was very hectic. People in aged Europe drink to taste the drink on their tongues. Here they drink to get drunk. We are brought up to gamble with finesse, for pleasure. But here they gather around the tables like people around bargain counters on dollar day. They lose their money without enjoyment.

Marjorie asked the cashier for five thousand dollars' worth of chips and signed a slip.

"Here. Take some," she said happily. "It's too much to carry around." She poured a stack of chips into my hands, then went quickly ahead to the tables and forgot about me at once.

I watched her for a few minutes.

Her face was tense, eager and expectant. For the first time she was not conscious of herself. Her expression was childlike, innocent, unsophisticated. This might have been her real self, but Marshall's school had taught her to be different.

I put my hand into my pocket and fingered the smooth, hard, ebony chips, fifty dollars apiece. I was carrying a thousand dollars around; fool's money, good only to be thrown away. I am no gambler. It bores me to win and I regret losing.

But the money in my pocket was not mine. She wanted me to gamble with it. She didn't mind if I lost all of it.

I suddenly got the idea of keeping it. I could tell her I had lost it. What difference would it make to her? None. And to me . . . a thousand dollars!

I felt like a pickpocket, and my heart began to thump. Cautiously, I turned around to watch her.

She sat at the roulette table. I went over to her quietly and looked over her shoulder.

Poor fools! How did they expect to win! The ordinary roulette in Monte or Paris Plage has one thirty-sixth advantage against the player . . . but this . . . here were two zeros and one eagle!

I put a chip on seven, *cheval, carré* and *transversale*.

She recognized my hand, turned and smiled, and went on, putting a stake on seven, too.

I lost my chip, and her money was raked in with mine.

That bored me. I walked over to the crap table with my nine hundred and fifty dollars.

I don't understand this game at all, and to conquer my desire to keep the chips, I put a hundred on eleven and promptly lost it.

A pity . . . one hundred dollars! How many times I could have taken Eleanor out with that. It would have paid the rent for three months and the milk bill for three years!

A small crowd sat around the table for chemin de fer, twenty-one, Russian Bank, or whatever they call it. A man who looked like a sleight-of-hand artist dealt the cards. He knew his cards as if they were transparent. It was no game of chance for him. He kindly let a poor extra win a few dollars, and then sniped a hundred-dollar bill from a feature player who had obviously just got his studio check and thought the future was secure.

I changed a fifty-dollar chip and lost the money quickly. Not one hand came up for me.

I still had five hundred and fifty dollars and, as is inevitable, I regretted having lost the money. To whom had I lost it? To the man who owned the club, who was making a quarter of a million a month . . . sucker money!

Marjorie was still sitting at the roulette table, a pile of chips in front of her. She had won! How strange! Could you really win against two zeros and one eagle?

I threw a chip on the table and played against her. I lost. Because I wanted the money, I had lost . . . and because it didn't make any difference to her, she won . . .

I went back to the crap table and put fifty dollars on eight. I lost. I had only one fifty-dollar chip left and I decided to keep it. It would pay for her rejected dinner.

She was still absorbed by the spinning wheel. I went to the rest room, to have my coat brushed and my shoes cleaned, my hands washed and the time killed.

The bouncer at the exit smiled benevolently at me. He perhaps already knew that the short visit had cost me nearly a thousand dollars. I was a welcome guest. Next time the wrought-iron gate would open without my name being asked.

The rest room looked like a high-class barber shop, with couches and deep chairs, and a couple of polite attendants who, along with hair lotions and perfumes, displayed Bromo-Seltzers and headache remedies. There should have been a doctor around for the more severe cases of roulette hysteria. People almost always feel sick when they leave a table with two zeros and one eagle!

The colored bootblack, after a quick glance at me, flashed an expansive smile. To him I seemed happy, like a man who had been winning. That meant a big tip. He didn't bother with people who were played out; they try to save on the bootblack what they have lost at the tables.

He moved his brush briskly, burnishing my shoes, while I watched my face in the mirror. Thin and pale, I looked rather distinguished in my tailcoat, I thought—like a San Franciscan whose ancestors have left him a few millions to toy with. As I expected to tip the boy heavily, I used some of the eau de cologne, and the nail file. While I was brushing my hair, I saw Jerry standing behind me.

Jerry was drunk. But in a quiet, desperate way.

"Hello, Jerry," I said, but he didn't return my smile. He pushed his hair back. His forehead was moist.

"What's the matter? Feeling bad?" I asked him. I was in a good mood, elated, walking on air—and his distress struck me as being funny.

"I feel lousy." He suddenly bent forward and put his head under the cold water, coming up dripping wet, his mouth hard, his eyes cold.

"Who hit you below the belt?" I joked. But he took a towel, rubbed his face and hair, and grabbed a brush and comb.

"Wait!" he ordered, as I turned to leave. I stopped. "I'm going to Frisco for a few days." He hesitated. "There are some things I've got to tell you and you've got to listen."

Frisco— If he had a job, he would be glad to brag about it; it couldn't be a pleasure trip, he didn't have the money. Suddenly it added up. He was working for

Marshall. I knew what was coming, but my good humor grew with his obvious distress. I slumped into a chair and watched him. My muscles tightened, prepared for anything.

He sat down, too, and took one of my cigarettes. "Damn," he said. "It's a mess . . ."

I waited, tried to make it easy for him.

"Marshall sent you?" I put my hand on his arm casually and patted him.

"I've been going around with him, since a few days ago . . ." Jerry said, and inhaled deeply.

"Well, bodyguard"—I smiled benignly—"shoot the works!"

"Look here, Pierre . . . for God's sake, be sensible. I've warned you . . . lay off his girl!"

"Did he send you to beat me up?" I leaned back gingerly. "Wouldn't that be a nice thing to do to a pal! Marshall must think a lot of you; more than of the two mugs he sent last time!"

"Pierre!" Jerry was distressed. Fundamentally, he was a nice boy. "I wouldn't stir a finger if you'd taken Robin, or the mulatto girl, or any of the others. But Marjorie Dean . . . do you know what you're getting into?"

"Jerry, my friend, I don't give a damn," I laughed lightly. "To tell the truth, I might laugh even if he put a few slugs in me."

He stared at me, frightened.

"I didn't know you were such a fool. Marshall . . . might even do that!" His voice dropped to a whisper. "Look—you don't know the circumstances, or you'd understand!"

"I'm not interested," I said, feeling very high and powerful. "Marjorie can do whatever she likes. She's over twenty-one, isn't she? . . . And *she* asked me to go out with her tonight, not vice versa . . ." It sounded like an excuse, and made it easier for him.

"Maybe she did," he said soberly. "But that makes no difference. She's worth too much to him . . . too much money to laugh off. He's found her, he's made her, he's running her life. And he'll fight anybody who comes between him and Marjorie Dean."

"Isn't he just the type to be in love with a girl!" I scoffed, visualizing Marshall's cynical face. "He looks like Romeo, doesn't he!"

But Jerry raised his voice angrily. "He's not in love with her. I'm telling you as a friend, Pierre, lay off . . ."

"Okay." I rose. "Thanks for the advice."

But Jerry pulled me down again.

"Sit down, you goddamn fool!" he said rudely, and I staggered back into the chair. "I'm going to tell you something. And you're going to stay here and listen!"

He stared wildly at me, prepared to hit me square on the jaw if I tried to get up.

"I don't care what you do, but I have to tell you . . . I have to get it off my chest. Marshall was a lawyer in New York. And somebody shot him in the groin, understand . . ."

He grabbed my wrist and pressed it hard, staring at me intensely.

"All right," I said. "Somebody shot him . . . I'm listening! But don't break my arm!"

His grip relaxed. "They took his license away. The bar commission, or whatever they call it, threw him out, so he couldn't practice any more. But he had some money. One night he went to a nightclub. And he saw Marjorie . . ."

He looked around, and said, "Damn, I need a drink . . .

my mouth is all dry . . ." He lit a cigarette and inhaled like a man breathing salt air.

"She was an unspoiled child—just sixteen then— and didn't know anything about anything. Her father used to call for her every night and take her home. Marshall bought her from her father. Heaven knows what he told the man, but he got her. Marshall had his plans all worked out. Are you listening?"

"Of course! Very interesting!" I said. "Just the right story to tell in a lavatory. Go on!"

"Marshall had his plan," Jerry repeated doggedly. "He wanted to make a pile! Steady money! She was beautiful—she still is—but then she had a quality of youth that drove everybody crazy. She was unsophisticated. She believed every word Marshall told her. He was careful with her. She really isn't different from any other girl and he was smart enough to know it. He never made a play for her. He slowly gained her confidence, concentrating only on grooming her for stardom."

He grinned in his twenty-eight-year-old wisdom. He looked wise and grave beyond his years, like a man who knows his own limitations. Jerry wanted Marjorie Dean but, since he never asked for anything he couldn't get, he made himself believe he didn't want her.

"Marshall had enough money to send her to the very best schools. You know—schools where girls are brought up in a fool's paradise—until they leave and discover the hell outside. I don't know how he forced the poor girl to go through all that. He made her really work. She speaks every language without an accent. She can sing and dance, and is educated in things Marshall has never even heard of. But that hasn't spoiled her. Marshall's bet was right. When he brought her to Hollywood, the studios went nuts. She was only eighteen when she signed her first contract. You know how they are—if they see something they can't buy, they get hysterical. And when two or three studios are bidding for the same thing, the sky is the limit. But they were clever, too. They sensed that Marshall was broke. And if they know that, then it's hard going. She didn't go up fast enough for Marshall. And Marshall knew she'd get to the top quicker if she married a star!"

"Niven!" I said, clairvoyant.

"Right on the nose!" Jerry was very friendly now. And, strangely enough, his drunkenness returned and he grinned amiably. "Niven married her fast. She was a juicy bit for a guy like him at forty-three. But, the way it happens with guys twenty-five years older than the girl, he lost his strength and his profile, and he began to slip. That's where the divorce comes in."

"And me," I nodded.

"Right!" He hiccuped very sociably. "Sorry—you! She asked for her divorce and a new contract. Marshall collects the dough and makes himself invisible. He's clever. You never see 'em go out together. She played her part well—and she's a hard mouthful to swallow. They couldn't make her budge. She got what she wanted. Parts, money, publicity, everything. She's got the big shots by the short hair. Now she's worth about a quarter of a million a year, and that's 50 percent for Marshall. She trusts him. And he keeps his grip on her. And now you—poor little worm—elbow in! He's getting frightened. Two hundred and fifty thousand dollars a year! Two hundred and fifty grand! Do you think he'll stand for it? . . . It's only human he's got it in for you!"

"I get it," I said, and felt very proud. "But just tell me—why should great big Marshall be afraid of little me? Hasn't Marjorie ever had an affair before? Does he expect her to live like a Mother Superior? You are at liberty to tell him, if it pleases you, that I haven't the slightest designs on her. She's not my meat, and he can keep her for good. I'm a strange guy, Jerry. I can't be bribed with money. I'm not a gigolo—not even a mental gigolo. Believe it or not! Send it to Ripley!"

Jerry looked at me in silence, thinking hard. He shook his head slowly. "Are you really that dumb? Marshall saw you cutting the sound track. You told the judge about it. Marshall had you beaten up. Now you turn up with her at this place . . . For God's sake, do you think he's a complete idiot? I'm telling you— scram! He's dealt with guys tougher than you!"

He rose and took one of his own cigarettes. Suddenly he looked up in alarm.

Only a few feet from us, Niven stood staring at me. I didn't know how long he had been standing there. Jerry turned at once and left without a good-bye. I stood up and said, "Hello!" There was nothing else to do. I couldn't ignore Niven's lunatic stare without making a fool of myself.

He smiled, and it was as if his features were breaking into small pieces like a jigsaw puzzle.

"My name is Niven." He stretched out a hand, cold and limp.

"Bernet," I said. "I saw you watching me while I danced with Miss Dean."

I wanted to get away. I was tired and upset. It was a futile game I was playing.

"Yes . . . Miss Dean . . . Marjorie . . . Marjorie . . ." He was lost in his thoughts at once, hypnotized by her name, and he repeated again—"Marjorie . . ."

Poor fool! He was all shot to pieces!

"What can I do for you, Mr. Niven?" I took his arm and led him away. I didn't want to talk to him about his love in a lavatory.

He followed me willingly, with the docility of a sick man. He didn't look up again. My kindness had loosened the strain. He hadn't expected to be treated with consideration. Men don't do that when there is a woman between them.

"Did you hear our conversation?" I asked casually, as if we were discussing the roulette table.

"Yes, sorry," he replied, ashamed that I showed no indignation about his eavesdropping and that he, a gentleman, had lowered himself to listen to a conversation in which he had no part.

We were walking toward the game room when he suddenly stopped.

"I'm very grateful to you, Mr. Bernet," he murmured and didn't lift his eyes. "You won't take offense if I ask you to have a drink with me at my house?"

"I'd be glad to," I replied, "if I can be of any service to you . . ."

We talked like two diplomats who discuss a delicate political situation without mentioning it at all.

"I didn't expect you to be so considerate," he said, then suddenly looked up with fear, pleading and desperation. "Tonight?" he asked.

"Tonight?"

Poor creature! He wanted to make sure that I didn't take Marjorie home and stay with her. He seemed to know her well, so his question was an eye-opener.

"Well—it's rather late . . . I don't think I could make

it tonight . . ."

He nodded, defeated. But he got himself in hand, and, like the gentleman he was, smiled with a gleam of the bravado for which his public loved him so much and his studios paid him so highly.

"Then be seeing you some other time."

He nodded like a king who greets the leader of the opposition, and walked off, his step elastic, his shoulders square.

12

I went back to the gambling room and looked for Marjorie. It was late, nearly two o'clock. After two we wouldn't be able to get any more drinks.

I found her at the baccarat table with a paper bag beside her. All the people around seemed to be exhausted except her. There were not many chips about.

She greeted me with an expansive smile. Under the harsh lights of the room she looked like a child who had been given permission to stay up late and was enjoying the treat. Among the professional gamblers, among the people who could find no other thrill than losing money, she was like a girl who had received an expensive present she hadn't expected.

"Hello, Pierre." She rose and grabbed the bag. "Take this." She pushed it toward me. It was heavy. We marched off followed by envious glances.

"What's in it? Nightshirt, toothbrush and breakfast?" I asked.

"Chips," she said. "Let's get rid of them. I couldn't keep from winning—at roulette, at the crap table, at baccarat . . . It's a big night. Good thing you don't love me—or I'd have lost!"

She held tight to my arm, keeping step with me.

"But I've lost your thousand bucks," I said. "I'm going to pay it back at the rate of a dollar and a half a week!"

"Okay—if you deliver the money yourself!"

We cashed the chips at the counter.

"Shall I write you a check, Miss Dean, or do you want cash?" the man behind the counter asked.

"Cash . . ." she said and opened her small bag to stuff it with notes. She couldn't even get out her lipstick now. She was like a charwoman taking home her daily vegetables. There was something coarse about her that the snobbish education at expensive finishing schools had not been able to erase.

"Off we go," she said.

"I want a drink," I said. "I'm all dried up!"

"You shall have three," she said generously. "But not here!"

"It's two o'clock . . . do you know a speakeasy?"

"Yes . . . the best one in town," she smiled at me and pressed my arm so that I could feel her breast.

"How strange! You're flirting . . . for the first time . . ." I said, and quietly took my arm away. "Until now you have been very matter of fact!"

"I always am . . . I'm old enough to make up my own mind!" She laughed coarsely. The laughter didn't suit her sweet face.

She turned to the hat check-girl and gave her a big bill. "Thank you, Miss Dean!" The girl stammered and curtsied and blushed. It was not the size of the tip that caused the blush, I was sure.

"Nice girl," Marjorie said to me. "Nice eyes!"

"Why don't you take her along?" I asked. I put her coat around her shoulders, while she carefully held onto her bag, changing it from her left hand to her right.

"No!" She was drunk without having touched alcohol.

Her car came sliding down the hill. I tipped the attendant a buck and felt the chip in my pocket. I had forgotten to change it. I wondered who had paid for the dinner.

"Where to?"

"Beverly Drive!" She moved to the far side of the seat, and I knew she was watching me. I stared straight ahead, feeling empty and disgusted.

"All right. I'll take you home!"

I speeded down Sunset at seventy. When I looked into the rear-vision mirror, I saw a car following us at the same speed. I slowed down to thirty, and the car behind did the same. It was not a police car, but a convertible two-seater. I dropped to twenty to let it pass, but the car behind drove the same speed. For a moment I was worried. Maybe Marshall's gangsters were already behind me?

"What's the matter?" She had sensed my apprehension and looked back. "Go on," she said harshly. "Don't bother!"

"Who is it?" I asked. She seemed to know the car.

"It's all right." Her voice was cold.

"Gangsters have big black closed sedans with two searchlights in front, if I remember right from the movies . . ." I said. But she didn't answer.

"Maybe somebody wants your autograph?" I scoffed. I knew she didn't want me to mention the car behind us. It was Niven's. I accelerated and got up to seventy-five, taking the corners with screeching tires.

When we arrived at her house, the pursuing car stopped a hundred yards behind us. I turned into the driveway, and stepped out. She sat there, somewhat apathetically.

"Tired?" I helped her out. She moved slowly.

"A little," she sighed.

"Good night, Marjorie. It was a pleasant evening!"

I was longing for a shower, for my bed, for the quiet of my room. But she seemed shocked.

"What about that drink?" She came so close that I could feel her breath. "You can't leave me like this!"

"Do you want to show me your etchings?" I tried to offend her, but it had the opposite effect. She put her arms around me and kissed me. I turned my face away. She broke loose at once and walked to the door. "Come on," she said, in a half voice.

I waited and lighted a cigarette. The two-seater had moved up opposite the house. I didn't want to talk to Niven now. I was too tired to face his unhappiness. It was easier to follow her than meet Niven.

That's why I went inside her house.

Lonza was still up. He took her coat. But he ignored me and left my hat on the chair where I had thrown it.

"Show Mr. Bernet to the bar, Lonza," she said, and walked away. I felt like a call girl, ordered in for an hour's entertainment.

Wordless, Lonza led the way to the bar. He resented my presence. That was unmistakable. Perhaps he had shown the bar to gentlemen too often. His black sense of propriety was offended. He served one of the most beautiful women in the world. He saw her oftener than most of her intimate friends did. It was only natural that he'd be in love with her. Consequently, every man who entered this house was his enemy.

The bar was a small intimate room—the walls painted with a view of the harbor, ships, houses, wharfs, and all. The bar itself was paneled in natural wood; its mirrored walls reflected dozens of bottles again and again, creating the illusion of a multitude of liquor flasks stretching limitlessly into space.

Lonza lit the fire in the fireplace and stepped over to the bar.

"What do you want to drink?" he asked gruffly. He had swallowed the "sir," and I had to put him in his place. I didn't like being snubbed by a servant.

"Nothing—and I don't need you any longer, either," I said, and turned to the fire.

He went out without a word and closed the door.

I switched off the lights. Only the fire lighted the room. I sat down and smoked a cigarette which I had taken from my pocket.

It was very quiet. I could hear the blood pounding in my ears. Something broke inside me, something like iron bands which had held my heart in bondage.

This was the turning point of my existence and I was aware of it.

I suddenly conquered my fear. It was fear that had poisoned my life. This fear suddenly disappeared, evaporated. Without obvious reason, it left me, like an evil spirit exorcised.

With infinite clarity I saw where I had come.

I was suddenly aware that I had no initiative whatsoever. I had as little personality as a baseball, which the strong and clever may send in any direction. Eleanor had got me where she wanted me. Joe had given me orders. Marshall had forced me to commit a crime. The judge had put me in my place. Niven expected something from me, something to his advantage only. And Marjorie left me waiting here in her bar until she was ready for the entertainment with which she wanted to end a pleasant evening.

I got up and paced the floor. It was impossible to leave now, without talking to her. I was no young Parsifal, fleeing from sin.

A Westminster clock struck half-past three. But time did not matter here in this timeless room with tightly drawn curtains.

I smoked another cigarette. It was the last I had with me. My mouth was dry, but I didn't want to pour myself even a glass of water.

When I looked up, Marjorie stood in the door.

She had changed into a Chinese kimono. Her skin was milk white, her hair loose around her shoulders. Like most women, she was more beautiful at night. She had never looked more alluring since I had first seen her.

"Hello," I said and sat down.

"Did you have your drink?" She walked over to the bar, shy as a little girl.

She was startled that I hadn't fallen to my knees in adoration. She had counted on that first impression, which had had no visible effect on me. Obviously she had known only pushovers.

"No thanks . . . no drink for me . . ." I threw the rest of the cigarette into the fireplace. "May I leave now?"

She sat down and folded her white hands in her lap. She was not used to refusals.

"What is the matter, Pierre? . . . I don't understand . . ." she asked timidly. The shyness was very becoming to her, and I couldn't help smiling.

"Why don't you call Niven? . . . He's outside . . .

waiting!"

"You're cruel. And you're a fool," she added and sighed.

"Remember our first conversation?" I said calmly. I wanted to end the scene. "You told me I was a fool then because I asked for something . . . and now, because I refuse, I'm a fool again. You like little games, don't you? Games where happiness or life itself is at stake. Because it's not your life, it's very amusing for you to watch. Are you aware of the consequences?"

"What consequences?" she asked innocently. She got up and stepped in front of me.

"Marshall . . . he sent word to me tonight to watch out . . . unless I wanted a free berth in the morgue . . ."

"You're afraid?" she asked. She raised her hand to touch my face.

I rose. "Good night, Marjorie . . ."

Suddenly she laughed and threw her arms around me and kissed me. I pushed her away and slapped her face.

She stood there, petrified, open-mouthed. I walked toward the door, feeling rotten and low, with none of the righteous anger that should have elated me. I could still feel her soft cheek burning against the palm of my hand.

She clung to my arm and trembled.

"Don't go . . ." she cried. "Stay here . . ."

I felt silly, walking along, dragging her behind me.

"Pierre," she cried, so loud that I expected Lonza to appear. "Pierre—you fool—you damned fool . . ."

Her gown had been pulled open. She wore nothing beneath it. She had prepared herself, sure of an easy victory.

We had arrived in the hall. My shirt tore in her

grasp. It was ridiculous to wrestle with a woman. What part was I playing? Young Joseph running away from Potiphar's wife?

I stopped.

"Sorry I hit you . . . now let me go . . ." I said quickly.

"No . . ." She held me tighter. Her hair had fallen into her face. Her strong white teeth were clenched like those of an epileptic. She was deadly pale, like a dope fiend who sees his "snow" being taken away, like a nymphomaniac whose lover is leaving.

"Pierre . . ." Her voice was choked. "Don't go—please—don't!" Her hand slipped through the shoulder of my torn shirt. Her body was pressed against mine. Her face was lifted. Her eyes were closed. I held her tight or she would have slipped onto the soft rugs which carpeted the hall. She sighed, half-conscious, her lips parted.

Her body . . . without restraint, soft, white and limp . . . I understood Niven and his infatuation. But had she ever shown abandon in his arms? I didn't know. And I didn't care about him. I forgot him, the world, tomorrow, and myself. I didn't care about anything but her.

13

It was bright daylight when I walked downstairs. The hall was quiet. Lonza and the other servants were still asleep. My battered hat was lying on the floor near the door. Two throw rugs showed the signs of last night's scuffle.

I threw the keys of her car on a chair. She had asked me to take the Cadillac and pick her up for lunch. She seemed to have made up her mind to carry on our relationship until the novelty wore thin.

She was one of those women who are grumpy and bad-humored in the morning. You have to feed them a hearty breakfast and light a cigarette for them before they are able to smile. They like to sleep late and, selfishly, think their sleep is more important than a polite good-bye. They behave in a way they would resent having men behave.

Unshaven, in tails and last night's white shirt torn at the shoulder, I felt like the waiter of a second-rate bar. The milkman was just walking up the red brick path to the back door. He called out cheerfully, "Nice morning, isn't it?" I resented his cheerfulness, which smelled of sarcasm.

Niven's car still stood opposite the house, its lights on. A crumpled figure was lying squarely on the seat, the head leaning against the window, one hand limply crossed behind the bent neck.

My heart stopped beating and I walked quickly toward the car. Perhaps Niven had killed himself, knowing I was in Marjorie's bedroom.

But he was asleep. His face was gray and sunken, his eyelids trembled, his breath came out of his half-closed mouth in small sighs. I watched his poor, tired face with morbid curiosity. Fool that he was, he had treated Marjorie like an equal. And now he was degrading himself by sleeping before her door like a dog.

He murmured. I couldn't hear what he said. But there was no hope for him. I saw his end written clearly on his forehead. Horses shy at a scene of murder even years after the occurrence. I have an unfailing premonition about the future. He was marked "To Die." He carried the same sign in his face that I have seen in my own.

I walked on—in the opposite direction, where he couldn't see me in case he woke now. It meant going two blocks out of my way, but I didn't want to be accosted by him.

To finish this episode in my life in style, I called a taxi. I still had three dollars and fifty cents in my pocket, and the fifty-dollar chip.

Suddenly I felt very tired, completely worn out. I examined myself in the glass of a window, and a seedy-looking face stared back at me.

We arrived at my apartment house, and the driver opened the cab politely and said, "One-ten." I gave him one-fifty. Rockefeller would only have tipped him a shiny new dime.

Al, the clerk, was already at work at the adding machine.

"Good morning, Mr. Bernet," he said with a twinkle, and took some slips of paper from my pigeonhole. "Coming home early? Hope you had a nice time!"

"One of the nicest," I said, and took the telephone messages.

Eleanor's number . . . Eleanor's number again. She had called four times during the night—at ten, at two, at half-past two, and at six. It must have been urgent, or she wouldn't have kept calling me all night.

I opened the door of my room and switched on the lights. Again I looked at the slips. Four calls! I suddenly felt faint. She needed me . . . the very night I hadn't been home!

I walked over to the telephone and took the receiver from the hook. But I put it back again. My heart began to beat so loudly that I felt its echo in my throat. The tempo increased, and I became panicky.

I sat down for a moment, trying to calm myself. That was it! Nothing had happened to her. If anything of real importance had happened, she would have called Joe, not me.

But at night? She couldn't call Joe at night, at his home. Maybe she wanted me to call Joe at night, because she couldn't!

I looked at the slips again and felt my forehead getting wet and cold. I read: "Mrs. Marr telephoned."

Mother Marr and not Eleanor! She had never called me before. Had Eleanor run away? Emily would know. Emily lived here in the building. Why not ask her? She might know for sure! I nervously clicked the house phone and asked for Emily. I was told she was working on a picture and had gone to Arrowhead for exterior shots.

I took the receiver and dialed Eleanor's number. There was no escaping it. I knew something had happened to her. I knew! My mind, trying to deny the truth, could not deceive me.

The phone rang about five times. I gave it another try, then hung up, and dialed the number again. This time Mrs. Marr answered at once.

"Hello," she said in a faint voice.

"This is Pierre speaking," I said and waited.

"Mr. Pierre," she answered, "I'm so glad you called . . . could you come over . . . now . . ."

"At once . . ." I said and hung up. I didn't ask. I didn't need to ask.

I threw the tailcoat in a corner and ripped the already torn shirt from my body. I flung my shoes to one side, but didn't take time to change the trousers. Getting my gray coat out of the closet, I grabbed a shirt and a tie at the same time and began to dress on my way out of the room. I had to stop at the elevator to button the shirt and put on the coat.

It was still early, but the noise of the first streetcar came clearly from Hollywood Boulevard. No taxi. There are no taxis in the morning, at this hour. No one would want a taxi at this time of day but me! I ran down Cherokee, praying for a taxi. None to be seen . . . none at the Boulevard, none in front of the drugstore. I should have phoned for one, but I had been anxious to lose no time. I couldn't run the whole way to Eleanor's house!

My mouth tasted of blood. My breath had given out. I stopped and waited. A truck came rolling along. I took a dollar bill from my trouser pocket and made a sign with my thumb. The truck stopped. I jumped into the driver's seat.

"Ten fifteen North Orange," I said, and followed with my eyes an empty taxi which had just overtaken us.

I pushed the dollar bill into the man's pocket.

"That's not necessary," he said and drove on. But he didn't give the money back to me. "You're in a hurry, aren't you?"

He speeded up to show his good will.

"What's up? Somebody ill?" he asked. I didn't answer, and he was sensitive enough not to ask again.

"I'm just coming in from Frisco, hauling stuff down," he said, to make up for his curiosity. And he gestured with his thumb toward the back of the truck. "Drove the whole night. A penny a mile and a buck for expenses isn't much!"

With this outburst, his eloquence was exhausted. He turned to the right at Melrose Boulevard. He knew this town well. When be rumbled up to Eleanor's bungalow, I opened the door and jumped out while he slowed down.

"Thanks!" I called, but he had already closed the door and was speeding away.

I found the front door ajar and entered. Fluffy, Eleanor's dog, was lying on a chair in the living room. His head was turned toward the curtain that separated the room from the rest of the bungalow. He looked at me and whined softly.

"They don't want you in there?" I asked and patted him. He moved his stubby tail and licked my hand. This was a moment when enemies become friends. Fluffy also seemed aware of that.

I sat down and waited. I didn't dare cross to the curtain. I didn't even dare call out that I was there.

A picture stood on the mantelpiece. It was a snapshot taken at the beach—Eleanor in a bathing suit against a white sky, smiling at me. I took it in my hands and looked at it, and put it into my pocket quickly when I heard Mrs. Marr enter.

"Hello, Pierre," she said gently and held out her hand. "Glad you're here. The child has asked for you often, but now she's asleep."

"What happened?" I was reassured by her calm. My fear had exaggerated the situation.

"It was rather bad. Glad I came home in time. I had gone out with Isabel, my cousin . . . but suddenly I was so worried about getting home that I couldn't enjoy myself. I had to go home! I knew something dreadful had happened. Only a mother knows things like that!" She looked at me for, understanding. I nodded impatiently, but I didn't dare interrupt her. She seemed to enjoy telling the story.

"When I opened the door, Eleanor was lying on her

bed, fully dressed, and moaning, her eyes closed and her hands clenched. I said to myself: 'Oh, oh! She's taken poison!' . . . Poison etches a line around the nose—here . . ." She touched my face with a cold finger. "I ran into the kitchen at once and warmed some milk. Then I called Dr. Abraham to bring the stomach pump. I opened Eleanor's mouth with a knife and poured the milk in. She had to swallow it, whether she wanted to or not. And then she began to throw up, and I knew I had guessed right. Then the doctor came and I helped him get the hose down, and we pumped the rest out.

"She had swallowed twenty-five tablets of veronal. Enough to kill a horse. And do you know where she got it? From my own medicine chest! I had saved that stuff for a long time, because I like medicines in the house. And she took all of them. Well, I'm glad it's over—now she's asleep."

She seemed well pleased with her own bravery.

"Why did she want to kill herself?" I asked. And the words choked me. A helpless expression suddenly clouded Mother's face.

"She's been quite strange lately. Something was the matter with her. But you know Eleanor—you can't ask her. If she wants to tell you, she will . . . if not . . ." She shrugged her shoulders resignedly. "While she was unconscious, she repeated your name . . . and another name, too . . . Joe. Do you know anybody by that name? She once had a friend called Joe, but that was three years ago. And he was just a kid. I don't think it's him . . . and she never talked about any other Joe. That's why I phoned you. Sorry I had to call you at night."

"That's all right . . ." Even in Eleanor's delirium I was second in her thoughts.

"Would you like to see her? She's asleep!" she said, and looked at me with empty eyes.

All her life Mother had lived with her daughter. But one day, maybe years ago, the child had cut herself free. One day Mrs. Marr had carelessly lost her daughter's confidence. And, instead of being confederates, they became companions, who exchanged stockings but no secrets. For a time this had been a smooth and easy way for Mother to live. It had suited her well, and she didn't notice that Eleanor had become a stranger to her. Millions of mothers live like that, carelessly getting rid of their children, cutting them out of the circle of their own lives, afraid to spend too much time and thought on them. They don't want to limit their own personal freedom.

And some day they find themselves as lonely as Mrs. Marr was at this moment.

"If she wakes . . . maybe she'll tell you . . ." Mrs. Marr said hopefully. I felt sorry for her.

"Maybe," I said evasively, and got up.

She rose, too, and staggered. I had to support her. I suddenly realized that all her bravado, her light passing off of the whole incident, was nothing but a carefully guarded front, a now transparent attempt to hide her loneliness and fear.

"I don't know what's in the girl's mind," she said helplessly. "I wonder why she did it . . . maybe she's in love!"

Desolately, she shook her head and moved toward Eleanor's bedroom. The door was open, and I saw Eleanor's light hair, her face hidden in the bend of her arm.

"I'll make you a nice strong cup of coffee," Mrs. Marr said. "You haven't had your breakfast yet, I'm sure . . ."

She shuffled away toward the kitchen as if this project had made her forget her daughter.

Quietly, I entered the room and sat down near Eleanor's bed. As if she sensed my presence, she took her arm away from her face and sighed. The green linen slip on the pillow in which she had buried her face made a faint shadow on her white cheek. Her lips were colorless. The line Mrs. Marr had talked of ran around her small nose. Her eyelashes, without the smudge of mascara, were as light as her hair; even her eyebrows were only faintly visible.

Even after swallowing poison, Eleanor could stand being observed by a man. She was young, just a child, who, at her first serious reverse, had thrown down her weapons at once and given up the battle of life. She was not weak; only inexperienced. It hurt me to think that she hadn't called on me for advice. Something dreadful had happened, or Eleanor, stubborn and positive, would never have taken this step.

Mrs. Marr came in and put down the coffee, toast and jam. She whispered something I didn't listen to, then walked out, closing the door.

I put my hand on the green pillow, close to Eleanor's mouth. She seemed to be awake, for she said, "Hello," in a whisper. She moved her cheek over onto my hand. I felt her measured breathing against my palm and bent forward so as not to disturb her. Had she recognized me?

This was a tiring position. My cramped back began to hurt. But I didn't dare move or take my hand from under her face. I put my other hand on her hair, and she smiled, without breaking the rhythm of her breathing. She moved her hand up and put it on my wrist.

This position was still worse. I had to smile at my predicament.

"Hello," I said. "Can you hear me?"

She gave no indication that she heard. I slid down to my knees, and did it without moving my wrists. That was quite a trick. Now I could relax a little and be even closer to her.

"Once upon a time . . ." I spoke close to her ear, "there lived in a hard and cruel country a hard and cruel man. He wasn't hard and cruel by nature. It was because, in order to make himself inflexible, he had had three iron bands forged around his heart. It felt fine, to be cruel and selfish. Nothing could touch him— no tears, no misery, none of the sufferings or troubles of wretched mankind.

"But one day he relaxed his guard and he fell in love. He couldn't help it, because he had taken no precautions against it, convinced that such a thing could never happen to him. His heart swelled, against his will, and he had no command over it. It hurt terribly. For the first time in his life he learned what pain meant. His heart was strong, and one after another it broke the three iron bands. That made a terrible noise in the silent night, and the girl he was with could not help hearing it. 'I didn't hear a thing'! he lied, when the first band broke. 'It must have been something outside . . .'

"'Well . . . something must be happening inside me ...' he confessed, when the second band burst. He was too selfish to admit that he was in love.

"'I love you,' he couldn't help saying after the third was gone. His heart was naked now, vulnerable as a lobster that had shed its shell . . ."

Her lips curled a little, but her breathing continued evenly: She only pressed her face deeper into my hand.

"Once upon a time there was a fish . . ." I continued. I put my head down on the bed. I was tired; my eyelids were heavy as lead. "The fish lived deep down in the sea, where no light can penetrate the water. He didn't need light, because he knew his way in the dark. He had a lot of company—fish with spotlights on their ugly foreheads, fish with luminous tails, big fish, prosperous fish, fish with big teeth and poisoned fangs. All were wild and bad, like our fish, who didn't know that the water would become lighter and friendlier the higher they went. He didn't know that there were birds flying above the water. And a sun was shining. And a moon and stars at night. Because he was a deep-sea fish and he had met only deep-sea fish, and he was afraid to leave his nice, dark night. His internal pressure was so great that it might burst him right open. He might fly into a thousand little pieces if he swam up there. He might spill out his soul, and all the birds would see it. How ashamed he would be, showing his soul to the birds. That's why he preferred to stay deep under the sea. He was just such a fish. But in his dreams he longed for the day when he would have courage enough to swim up there to see the birds and the real light—for once. But he knew he'd die instantly!"

She moved her hand and put it against my lips. I closed my eyes, and my mind wandered off.

14

I thought I had only closed my eyes for a minute. But in my dazed and foggy mind I heard a clock striking again and again, unendingly. It was twelve—noon.

I straightened my stiff neck. Eleanor was still asleep. My feet were numb and it took several minutes before I felt the prickling sensation of returning life in them. I drank the cup of cold coffee which stood on the small table near the bed. The saucer clinked a little when I put the cup down. This small clatter woke Eleanor.

She looked at me as through a mist, eyes straining with uncertain focus. Her iris changed size like that of a cat staring into the light.

"Pierre," she said, and her voice was hoarse. "I didn't know you were here . . ." She stretched out her hand and I took it quickly.

"Just relax," I said. "Don't think, don't talk, and don't wonder . . ."

"When did you come? Have you been here long?" she tried to concentrate, but gave it up. She had forgotten that I had talked to her a few hours ago. It had been only an instinctive reaction to my voice when she smiled. As people in a coma smile when they hear other people laugh. It was better for her that she had forgotten my silly stories. It made it easier for both of us.

"Mother called me just a few minutes ago," I said lightly, and succeeded in deceiving her. "She thinks it's encouraging for a girl to find a man sitting by her bed when she wakes."

She tried a little smile.

"I've an awful taste in my mouth," she said, and reached for a glass of water which stood on the small table. I passed it to her, and she took a sip, made a face and said, "Awful—like medicine—what is it?"

"Water!" I answered. "Haven't you heard of it . . . they say it tastes lousy."

She turned on her back and buttoned the pajama at her throat. She tried hard to sort out her thoughts.

"I swallowed that stuff," she said thoughtfully. "That's what it is . . . I hate to swallow pills . . ."

"There was once a woman who gulped down twenty-five veronal tablets, three grains of strychnine and half a pound of cyanide. And she damned near killed herself," I said and knelt down beside her.

"Dr. Abraham was here," she remembered. The night began to unveil its contours. "He hurt me . . ."

"But not enough," I said. "You should be spanked for frightening your friends and keeping your poor mother up the whole night, and not even giving me time to shave."

"I can't live any longer, Pierre," she said gravely and sincerely. "It's no use!"

"A fine crack, after all the trouble we've gone through!" I smiled and felt a lump in my throat. "But I'll make a bargain with you. If you can convince me that you have a good reason for calling it quits, I'll help you do it quickly and on a one-way track."

She stared at me listlessly and said in a small voice: "Mrs. Sherman was here last night."

I nodded quickly and patted her hand. Why hadn't I thought of that!

"I expected it all the time . . . didn't you?" I spoke with false astonishment at her desperation. "I should have warned you. She was sure to show up here someday. But what of it?"

"She doesn't want a divorce any more . . . she withdrew it!" Eleanor said in despair.

"It's obvious . . . she would do a thing like that. It's just a trick to raise her price . . ." I held her hand tightly, but she shook her light hair. "Oh no . . ." Her voice was scarcely a whisper. "She told me she's going to stick to Joe . . . until we both crack . . ."

"Don't be frightened," I said. I was aghast. Eleanor defenseless against that concierge from Neuilly.

"She said she had withdrawn the divorce suit for good!" Eleanor told me. I nodded encouragingly. She needed to tell me everything, to get it out of her system, to clean up this mess. "She said I was a prostitute. And she spat in my face, and shouted so loud I was afraid the neighbors would come in. It was horrible, Pierre . . . what could I have done? She was so horrible and ugly and unkind . . . There's no way to fight her . . . I know she'll never give up . . . never . . . never . . ."

If it were possible, she grew paler. Her mouth trembled. Suddenly she began to cry. Her frail body shook in my arms. I wanted her to cry; it would relieve her.

I waited a few minutes, and felt like a doctor watching his patient.

"Okay. Snap out of it!" I said harshly after a while. "Stop crying now. Don't be silly! That old cow was only jealous because you're young. She's finished and her only satisfaction is to insult you. She wanted you to do just this! It would make everything perfect for her! You should have brains enough to know that! She enjoyed the scene. She got a big kick out of it. And she hoped you'd fall for it!"

Eleanor stopped crying at once; a ray of hope dawned in her eyes. She stared at me and reached out her hand to touch my face.

"Are you sure?" she asked. But her voice gave out.

I produced an impatient sigh and tried to be very matter of fact about the whole terrible incident. I know that type of woman. She'd never give up. She'd enjoy the melodrama to the last scene. She would live a full life at the side of a man who wanted nothing more than to get rid of her. She knew that Joe would never leave her without a proper divorce. Eleanor's reaction to Mrs. Sherman was right. There was no way to fight this woman.

"Why didn't you call me before you took the pills? It's not very fair to me, is it? Or to Joe, either . . . Now you have to stick it out. You can't leave Joe like that, and you know it! He'd never survive the shock!"

She nodded earnestly. "I couldn't help it . . . I was so alone. I couldn't phone Joe . . . and you weren't in . . . and then . . . I didn't know what to do . . . I was so tired all of a sudden . . ."

"That's a woman's logic," I said. "Because you were tired, you took a handful of sleeping pills!"

I was relieved to have dragged her away from her dark thoughts. But how did I know they wouldn't return? Another week . . . or two . . . one more scene like the one last night, and she would try again and succeed. I had to talk to Joe about it.

"I wonder what would have happened if I had killed her last night," she said suddenly. And the desperate look came back into her eyes. "It wouldn't have been murder. It would have been a . . . how do you say it . . . ?"

"*Crime passionale* . . . but not quite!" I laughed. And

my heart began to flutter as if it had been touched by an ungentle hand.

"You look pale, too," she said, aware of me for a moment. But she forgot about me at once. "Oh, Pierre, what can I do? . . . I can't stand it . . ."

She thought of herself all the time. Of nothing but herself! She was all that mattered. She was so absorbed in herself that she had tried to throw her life away just because it didn't run the way she wanted. But she was in love; that's why she was to be forgiven.

"Let me talk to Joe . . ." I said. And I bent down and kissed her forehead. "Maybe this scene last night is a good excuse for his getting a divorce. Just give me time . . . a few days . . . And promise you won't do anything silly again without telling me first . . ."

"Promise." She smiled with complete faith. Her eyes were warm and kind. I loved her so much it was physical pain.

"See you soon!" I said. She didn't answer. Her eyes followed me to the door. I saw her lying there in bed, smiling at me confidently as I left.

She went out of my life as she had entered it—with a smile and a hope for tomorrow.

I've never seen her again.

15

I walked up Melrose, went into a barber shop, and spent my last dollar for a shave, a haircut and a shoeshine. I felt all right and was ready to play Cupid.

I didn't dare think of my own situation. I was standing outside the periphery of happiness. Who ever thought of me? I was the postman who delivered the registered letter with the money inside . . . And I got nothing for it but a hurried "thank you."

To shorten the time and distract my mind, I bought a paper. On the front page, beside the headline which told of the destruction of Boulogne, but in print three times as high, I read that the Niven-Dean decree had become final. For the sake of symbolism, Niven's and Marjorie's pictured faces were turned away from each other. Mr. Niven scowled at the left side of the page. Miss Dean smiled at the right. The decree was given on grounds of mental cruelty—her mental cruelty, actually, I suppose, but the paper said just the opposite.

I remembered Niven's tired, sunken face. He had exhausted his life, had no reserves to draw from. As I felt helpful, like a trained nurse, today, I made up my mind to visit him too, after I had talked to Joe.

The World Film Laboratory Corporation was still in existence. It seemed years since I had been there. Time is relative because we are able to think in only three dimensions. The fourth cannot be understood by our limited intelligence. But, as we travel on an ever-shifting plane, the fourth dimension sometimes edges into our consciousness and we seem to have already lived through the present moment.

I knew I had entered this house before at this precise moment. I knew that a page of an old newspaper would lie just inside the door, folded so that it's back was to me. A voice would call from upstairs. I couldn't recall what it said, but I remembered the intonation distinctly. A door would open and a woman leave. But I couldn't recall her features.

And so it was. The three-dimensional time arrived at the point which I had lived through before. There was the voice, the folded paper, and the woman, who opened the door of the World Film Laboratory Corporation. She was just the person I didn't want to see: Mrs. Sherman!

She hadn't expected to see me either. And she was visibly surprised, but pleasantly so. Because when she recovered from the shock, a smile appeared behind her Indian make-up and conveyed, in a distorted way, a faint reflection of her former loveliness.

"Oh ... M. Bernet ... comment ça va?" she exclaimed, and went on in English. "Did Mr. Sherman expect you? He is not at home!"

"Well," I said, and smiled, "I don't mind. Do you?"

Women seem to sense it when a man has had an affair with another woman a short time before.

She wiggled, shifted from one foot to another, and gave me a friendly once-over.

"But I really don't know when he'll be in ..."

"Oh ... Then it's no use waiting. Thank you so much, Mrs. Sherman."

My expression must have betrayed my relief at not finding him at home. Unconsciously, I was glad not to have to talk to him. This genuine reaction, which did not escape her, pleased her.

"He might be back soon," she said. "Why don't you come in?" And she opened the door wide. I wanted to say that I didn't think I could wait. When I looked at her again, I felt I couldn't stay, but in spite of my feelings, I walked in.

She was dressed in a tailor-made suit and a white blouse with lace around her fat neck. She even wore a small toque on her platinum hair. The hat was incongruously elegant and didn't suit her concierge outfit. Still on the warpath, she had made herself ready for another ambush.

Again the perfect organization of Joe Sherman's office impressed me. Even the chairs had been lined up with ruler and triangle. I could imagine her in her fury against this man she couldn't reach. She would push the chairs out of place, throw paper all over the floor, upset the inkstand, and soil the room as much as possible, until she calmed down, sobbing. And he, with his saintly patience, would tidy up again, never complaining at all. That was the fiendish part of his revenge. She wanted to hear him shout. She wanted to be beaten, kicked . . . But his quiet lack of any reaction had driven her close to insanity.

I looked at her with curiosity and began a friendly conversation.

"Madame is from France?" I asked. "From what part?"

"Paris," she answered in the hard accent of a Rumanian.

There is nothing more irritating to a Frenchman than a Balkan accent. The English accept a mispronunciation of their language good-humoredly. The Germans find it smart to have a foreign accent. But the French are intolerant . . . Their language is their treasure, and even the lowest street cleaner tries to speak it with perfection. And a foreigner, mauling the beautiful diction, mispronouncing the treasured words, becomes at once an enemy, loathsome and deadly.

We sat quiet for a moment. She had crossed her legs to show her very small shoes. Her foot was out of proportion to the leg; a foot my grandfather would have admired. It was so small that I looked at it with real curiosity. She sat without moving; she knew what she was showing. It was her ace card, the only part of her that hadn't changed since she was a slender girl.

"Where do you have your shoes made?" I asked her. "They're adorable!"

This was the nearest thing to a compliment I dared to utter without giving away my dislike for her. My caution, which she interpreted as embarrassment, pleased her no end. It confirmed her belief that here sat a man who admired her, who could understand her personality, and who appreciated her charms. I understood her so well that none of my moods were false or made her suspicious. With delicate precision I walked the tightrope that led to her confidence.

She didn't talk, but watched me. I cast down my eyes in boyish confusion. And her feminine instincts, long suppressed and tortured into unhappiness and slyness, rose again from the junk pile of her personality.

"I heard you've been ill," she said. I didn't know where she had heard it. Joe couldn't have told her. And in order to show my confidence in her discretion, I nodded demurely.

"Yes," I said. "We are in a country where we don't belong and which doesn't understand us."

This shot hit the bull's-eye, and her eyes melted.

"You seem to feel like I do," she said. "I've been here for more than twenty years. And there's not one day I haven't dreamed myself back to the little *bistro* at the corner of Avenue Friedland and Rue Tilsit."

She might have been a waitress at this place. There are a million *bistros* in Paris, and this one may have been her home. Her dream was to stand behind a counter selling *brioches* and *croissants*. I sighed, to show that my thoughts, too, dwelt in the corner *bistro*, the heaven of happiness.

I was following a plan which at the time wasn't clear to me at all. Intuition guided me—to what goal, I couldn't make out. My temperature was low, like that of a sick man the doctors have frozen to relieve his last hours of the agony of pain. But my mind worked like a clock, without affecting my feelings. I had no reaction of joy or fear, discontent or hope. This woman had to be caught. And she was attracted to me like a cat by the smell of valerian.

"Oh—please don't talk about my Paris," I said, like a man in an old-fashioned melodrama. It was thick, but she took it, and her eyes became moist.

"How right you are—what's the use?"

Before she could pour out more of her liquid emotions, I beat a retreat and stammered: "Would you mind . . . if I asked you . . . but I shouldn't . . . because you're a married woman . . . but I'm so lonely in this town . . ." I stopped with false embarrassment. I didn't want to give it to her all in one sentence.

"Yes, Mr. Bernet?" she asked encouragingly. She anticipated what was coming, but she was afraid I wouldn't find the courage to finish my sentence. If she had had only one grain of that sympathy last night, at Eleanor's . . . the future would have taken a different course.

"I dread the empty evenings. This coming home with no one waiting. The lonely meals at unfriendly drugstore counters! Mrs. Sherman, would you be very much offended if I asked you to have dinner with me . . . . just out of kindness? I'd appreciate it tremendously!" I said, with a tremolo.

"Of course, Mr. Bernet . . . I'm very lonely, too!" She moved her upper torso forward and came quite close to me with her enormous breasts. I rose at once.

"Tonight, *chérie*," I said. This was the test. *Chérie!* Would she accept the word? Would she become suspicious at this forward attack? No . . . nothing like that!

"At nine o'clock, at La Brea and De Longpre," she murmured and rose too. We didn't look at each other again. I rushed out. I didn't want to see her face, and she took my haste for shyness.

She must have had the impression that I was naive. What she wanted was someone she could dominate, someone she could bully. Joe she could not. He was unapproachable, the nearest thing to a Biblical saint that ever existed. I'm sure he hadn't even talked to her for years. There was no use in her screaming, shouting, crying, destroying things, making any sort of scene. There was no use in being kind to him, considerate or obedient. He had closed that chapter of his life . . . and buried it. For him she no more existed than last autumn's leaves. He had locked the iron gates of his citadel, and she was left standing outside. She had tried again and again to enter, then given up, and agreed to the divorce.

Until the day that she found out about Eleanor. Here it was, his Achilles' heel! Here she could mortally wound him!

She went to the girl and told her everything she had to say. She cut loose, and she had a lot to tell. It was like the eruption of Mount Pelée . . . it would have wiped out stronger girls than Eleanor. It had pushed her close to the edge of the precipice.

Now she'd never leave Joe, now that she knew about Eleanor! What a beautiful life lay before her! How she would enjoy torturing Joe until he broke down!

But she still didn't mind having a little fun on the side. She had a date with me.

This was the flaw in her plan. She was so swollen with victory that she had forgotten to establish lines of communication. She had become callous and overconfident.

I left the building as Joe stepped out of his car. He moved slowly and shut the door carefully, like a nurse closing the door of a sick man's room. His face was sad and his steps unsteady.

When he saw me, his face lighted.

"Mr. Bernet," he said, and pressed my hand. "I tried to get in touch with you. I should have guessed that I'd find you here at my office. You came to see me . . . thank you . . ."

Instinctively, we walked away from the World Film Laboratory Corporation.

"She is all right. It was an awful shock to her. She's only a child." He nodded.

"My . . . wife told me last night that she had seen Eleanor. I tried to phone her. There was no reply. I couldn't go to her myself; it was impossible. I hoped and prayed Eleanor would have the strength to see it through. I tried to protect her from the dirt this woman has thrown at her. I tried to strengthen her for this day. But it came before I was ready!"

For the first time he was helpless. He took my arm, and his religion, on which he had relied at every crisis of his life, forsook him now. He was no saint; he was filled with fear like any other human being.

"Eleanor is all right. I've talked to her. I just came from her. She is confident and strong. She knew that I was coming to see you, and she asked me to reassure you. She'll wait as long as you wish. She told me that . . ."

He didn't answer, but he got himself under control again.

We walked along in silence, until he remembered that I was with him.

"And you?" he asked, slowly and painfully. "And you, Pierre?"

I could have cried. What the hell was he asking me that for?

"Me . . . what do you mean?"

"You're in love with her, too," Joe said simply. "Forgive me for mentioning it. What're you going to do?"

"Thanks for asking me, Joe," I said. My throat ached as if I had cried too much. "My problem isn't very difficult. She's not in love with me . . . she loves you. What can I do about it? The only strength I have is the power pride gives me. I'd rather break than admit my feelings to anybody but you. Maybe I like being tortured. That's what I'm still trying to find out. But isn't it better to look the facts in the face than be deceived and find it out later . . . too late?

"I trusted a woman once, the only real love of my life, and she betrayed me all the time. But she betrayed the other man, too! With me! Even when she came from him her eyes didn't show any feeling for him. I couldn't discover the slightest shadow of a memory in them. That affair finished me for years. My soul dried up, my feelings shriveled. When I looked at anything beautiful, I did it with the purpose of finding flaws, of hurting it, of hating it. That's what that woman did for me. The moment she felt she was happy, she had to destroy. But, unfortunately, she did something so unkind that it extinguished my love for her like a fire that is treated with chemicals. At the same time the memory of a few true moments of love died, too. There was nothing left. In retrospect, everything which had been beautiful between us left a bitter taste in my mouth.

"After I came to Hollywood, I met Eleanor, and I lived through the same hell again. I waited for her telephone calls. I waited for hours. I didn't leave my room for fear she might call. I thought over all the inconsistencies of her conduct, weighing every word she ever said which sounded like encouragement. Honest, in her blunt way, she told me about you at once. She is hard, but clean. She doesn't know how cruel she is. No one has told her.

"But still . . . I don't want to give her up. I tried to fit the missing parts into the puzzle. I tried to imagine what happened when I wasn't with her . . . the things she purposely concealed in order not to hurt me. All this is agony, continual hell. It hurts like a pain in the head that only a major operation can cure.

"I am in love with her . . . how can I help it? There's no use fighting; she has settled everything. She is in love with you . . . forever. Please, Joe, don't make it any more difficult by asking me questions. Don't make me break down. Leave me the last thing I have left— my pride."

I had talked rapidly, and all the time I was speaking to him I wanted to stop but couldn't. I couldn't dam the flow of my words, and when I finally clenched my teeth, I was exhausted.

We still walked on. He had taken my arm and didn't reply.

"Where are you going?" he asked.

"Home," I said.

"I could give you a lift . . . " he said. We stopped.

I looked into his eyes. We didn't have to speak. We

looked at each other for some time. Then he nodded.

"Good-bye, Pierre." He held out his hand and I took it.

"Good-bye, Joe," I said, turned and walked away.

16

I cashed a check at Schwab's and bought a bottle of Pernod, some charged water, flowers, and cold food for dinner. It was about five when I entered my room.

I set the table for dinner. The sight of the food revolted me, so I took a drink, straight. Afterwards I changed to my blue suit, white shirt and my only blue tie. It was frayed at the top and needed artful tying.

My bankbook was hidden in the top drawer of the desk. I took it out and looked at it. There had once been more than a thousand dollars in it, the slow accumulation of a few dollars every week. Now it was whittled down to eighteen dollars and fifty cents.

I took a pen and, imitating the flowery script of the bank clerk, I added five hundred and fifty dollars, and fixed the date. On the next line I added another twelve hundred, then eighteen hundred. Playfully, I rounded the sum out to four thousand and twenty dollars and forty-five cents. It looked pretty genuine. I put the chip from the Club Femina on top of the book and locked the drawer, but left the key in its hole.

With this finished, I had one more errand to do. I had to see Niven.

The clerk at the desk had given me three messages. All three were from Marjorie. I threw them into the wastebasket. It was good for her to have a man behave as she usually did, for a change. There was nothing to make me want to repeat last night. She was too selfish; only concerned about her own pleasure. I was disgusted.

I picked up the house phone and told the clerk: "If Miss Marjorie Dean calls, please tell her I'm not in!"

"Yes, Mr. Bernet," the clerk whispered in awe.

The newspaper had fallen out of my pocket and Niven's picture looked up at me. I threw the page away, and after a last survey of my kingdom I left. I was satisfied. It looked like the room of a bachelor who expects the sweetheart of his dreams.

As I walked out to Beverly Hills, I remembered the day I had gone to see Marjorie. It was an eternity ago! It was yesterday!

I knew I had stepped onto a toboggan which was speeding to the finish line with increasing momentum. I enjoyed the ride. The wind whistled around my ears, the air became colder every moment, but I was still steering this thing skillfully. I would crack up at the finish, but the ride was worth it.

Night had fallen quickly. I hadn't even realized how late it was. Sometimes I'm wrapped in my thoughts, and when I look around again the clock has moved a few more hours without me.

I walked along Rodeo Drive, looking out for a police car to give me a lift. But it was too early for the cops to be roaming about; they like to pick their people up late.

I had never been so busy in my life, galloping from one important rendezvous to another, fighting half a dozen battles in a day, with more still to come. Life was fascinating.

Sometimes, in a quiet moment, I thought it was a little too fascinating, even for a man who had nothing to lose.

I walked slowly, for I had time on my hands. My date with Mrs. Sherman was at nine.

I didn't even know her first name. I'd call her chérie, instead of Magdalene, or Angela, or whatever her name was.

Niven lived at the Vista del Mar apartments. As a matter of fact, they only look out onto gardens; the ocean is twenty-two miles away. But here things often have names which mean just the opposite. Thus a weenie bake takes place at the beach, and a picnic, called a fish fry, can only be served in the woods. That's why, perhaps, the Vista del Mar apartments have a vista of nothing but trees.

It was an imposing arrangement of fashionable bungalows, set in a square, facing each other like grenadiers. Very modernistic, with wide windows and flat roofs, they were the last word in elegance.

The square was deserted and almost completely dark. In one house all the lights were ablaze, as if a big party was on.

It was Niven's bungalow.

The silence was strange. Not even the noise of the faraway town was perceptible. Ordinarily, you hear the town almost everywhere. It makes the air vibrate like the faint humming of a broken pipe organ.

But here even the air seemed to be soundproof.

I knew I'd get a drink or two at Niven's. And the idea of a long glass with ice cubes, charged water, and whisky pleased me.

I'd listen to Niven while I sipped my drink. At the end of it, I'd say to him: "Sir, let's talk frankly, as one gentleman to another. You're mistaken! You think that everyone who has slept with this beautiful woman is infatuated with her. Please be assured—nothing of the sort has happened to me. I didn't take anything from her, because whatever she gives she takes back quickly. She is what you call an Indian giver.

"I didn't break anything either. This very solid piece of beautiful china is still uncracked. I drank a cup of tea out of it, but that's what the cup was made for. Wash it, and it's like new. I have no designs on her—I assure you again. But if you see the slightest chance of getting her back again, please don't hesitate. This woman understands plain English.

"I won't stand in your way. But if you'll take a piece of advice—don't go near her! It doesn't pay. It will make you very unhappy. It might even finish you. So, if you're a man, forget it. It may hurt a little at first; nobody can deny that. But plenty of other women have similar qualities." Actually I didn't expect to accomplish very much. When a man has sunk as low as Niven, verbal calisthenics don't help. There wasn't anything that I could say to him that he hadn't said to himself, and, in the final analysis, had lost the argument. But I wanted to talk to him. It might possibly help.

I rang the bell and waited. No one answered. I pressed the button again, and listened. Nobody home! All right. I didn't care!

Pricked by curiosity, I pushed the handle. The door was not locked. Niven was certainly insured against theft, as rich people always are. I peered inside. In the hall a print of Van Gogh's *Sunflowers* hung over a gray rug, red furniture stood in front of a big fireplace, which was hammered brass. Nice house to live in!

I cleared my throat loudly. Nobody in! I threw my hat on a chair next to the door and walked inside, bolder, and with increasing curiosity.

Next to the hall was the dining room, quite nicely furnished in American maple. The kitchen seemed to come next, but I didn't open that door. A Filipino might be sleeping behind it. There was no other room downstairs. There seemed to be one bedroom upstairs, and a library, and the servants' rooms in the back of the house.

The whole atmosphere was impersonal. A department store had sent all the furniture, ordered by telephone: "Please furnish my house," Niven might have said. "I want to spend so much. Just go ahead and do what you like . . . " But it's not only the furniture that makes a house. It's the personal touch, which you can't buy with money.

Well . . . I still had plenty of time on my hands. And instead of roaming the dark streets, I might just as well wait here. Niven might come home any time.

Slowly, I walked upstairs. The gray rug swallowed the sound of my steps.

On the next floor, from which a balcony overlooked the hall, the lights were on, too. The door to the library was open. Nobody there . . . A concealed bar with open doors. A glass and a whisky bottle stood on the polished wood of the bar. The floor was soiled with ashes and innumerable cigarette butts.

I coughed again and was bold enough to call out: "Hello . . . "

No answer! Silly to leave the house with all the lights on! The door to the next room was open. It was the bedroom. The bed had been slept in lately; its pillows lay on the floor. It looked like a room left in haste. Since it was evening now, why had this room been left disarranged in this meticulously kept house?

Niven should fire his servant!

I stepped inside the room and stopped short, as if I had run against an iron railing. A screaming terror gripped me; I couldn't move my eyes, my head, or a single limb; I was forced to stand and stare!

In the middle of the bathroom, Niven's body was lying, clad in pajamas. The whole bathroom was smeared with a dark-brown color, with whitish stuff sticking to the walls and ceiling. Where Niven's head had been, there were formless masses of hair and gray matter and a featureless face. Near the body lay a gun—a long-muzzled weapon, presumably a Colt.

I stared until I felt faint. Maybe I had fainted, but I still stood on rigid legs. I turned and walked down the stairs, then began to run when panic caught up with my numb brain. I raced through the garden, out onto the street and down toward Sunset. At a corner I stopped, ashamed of myself.

He was dead—what was I afraid of?

But I trembled. My hands were cold and moist. I was responsible for his death! I, but for my laziness, could have saved him. He had waited outside Marjorie's house. And then he had gone home, found the paper with the announcement of the final decree, saw her picture in the newspaper, and ended his journey of pain and desperation.

He was the first corpse I had ever seen. I didn't know that a body could make such a terrible mess on floors, walls and ceiling. He had obviously filled the gun barrel with water and fired into his mouth, to be sure not to fail.

I walked on, when suddenly I remembered that I had left my hat. My hat was still lying on the chair in the hall, with initials and cleaner's marks and the

French label: Tuellet, *chapeaux fins*, Paris. In a few hours the police would arrive, find the hat, look for me at once. And I'd have a lot of explaining to do that wouldn't sound very convincing. I had to go back and get that thing!

I waited a few minutes before I turned back.

If I didn't go back for the hat, I was sure to make the headlines. Hadn't this been my burning wish only a few days ago? Here was my chance: FRENCH FILM CUTTER AND MARJORIE DEAN MOTIVE FOR NIVEN'S SUICIDE! How she and Marshall would love that! She'd be finished in Hollywood.

I went back to the house like a man who chooses to walk to his execution. I was a coward, a fearful little mouse, without guts, frightened into a blue funk. The lights were still ablaze. I stopped and watched. Nothing seemed to have changed. Niven hadn't been found yet. There was no danger . . . I could sneak in and grab my hat and walk away. Who would know? Niven had reason enough to go to hell, without my help.

It would take only a second—the door was still open.

I stepped inside.

The hat was gone! I knew I had thrown it on the chair. It had been there before. On the chair! But there was no hat on the chair, nor under it, nor anywhere in the hall. Maybe it had flown upstairs. Maybe it had jumped right into the bathroom and was nestling close to the mangled brain of the dead man? Maybe it was soaked with blood and slime. My initials were in it, and the name of the Paris hatmaker!

Someone had taken it away!

I walked out of the house. I didn't have courage enough to go upstairs. I might have taken it to the library. You never remember positively where you have left things. But I couldn't face the bedroom door, and the awful silence.

I hid behind the bushes at the side of the garden walk, and jumped over the wall. This was safer than walking out the front way. The earth was soft. I sank into the ground up to my ankles and waded slowly through the mud toward the street.

Suddenly I saw them again—Marshall's friends: the man with the cauliflower ears and the nose that pointed toward his left shoulder, and the thin fellow with the reddish hair. They were standing across the street, waiting. A car was parked nearby. And a man with a small mustache sat there at the wheel. All three looked toward the stage, the Vista del Mar apartments. They were talking to each other, and the red-haired one ran toward the square, while the cauliflower man held my hat in his hand and turned it around, curiously.

I pulled back slowly, carefully. I didn't stampede. I found a taxi one block farther down,

17

I asked the driver to take me to La Brea and De Longpre. I tucked myself deep into the seat in order not to be recognized by the three boys. Marshall had sent them to bring me in, dead or alive. He certainly regretted now that the "traffic accident" he had staged hadn't been more successful. I knew too much about Marjorie, about him, about his affairs. He didn't know that I didn't care, that I wasn't even curious anymore; he only knew that this wasn't a simple divorce case anymore, a friendly parting, with plain alienation of affection and ordinary "mental cruelty." The Federal authorities might step in now and take the thing out of Marshall's hands. Hence the urgency of stopping me—the key witness. Even if nothing was proved, the scandal would ruin Marshall's precious source of income.

You can do whatever you like inside your house, but the outside must be kept whitewashed. Public opinion is the strongest and most relentless judge. And Marshall was deadly afraid of it. He wanted to stop me . . . now!

The toboggan raced on at top speed and I had to hold tight not to be thrown off before the finish.

The taxi stopped at the corner of De Longpre. I opened the door and waited without getting out. It was still twenty to nine, but Mrs. Sherman stepped out of the dark. Quickly, she entered the cab.

"*Bon soir*, Pierre," she said and giggled. She was excited. She hadn't had an adventure for a long time, I suppose.

"Yucca and Cherokee," I told the driver. And at the same time I pressed Mrs. Sherman's hand, which, soft and fat, felt like a small pillow.

"I'm early, chérie . . . I have been waiting for this moment so impatiently . . . I didn't want to miss a second, in case you should arrive early," I said in my deepest, most persuasive voice, adopting a strong Parisian accent. We spoke French from now on and she relaxed, pleased with her success. She forgot that she had been early, too.

"I shouldn't have come," she said, "but it was such a relief that you asked me . . . it was like a voice from Paris . . .!"

"Bucharest," I wanted to say, but kept silent again and pressed her hand. I could feel the little dimples on the back of her fingers, though I couldn't see in the dark of the moving car. I dislike hands like that.

"Chérie," I began and stopped. I didn't know what to say to her. She was too clairvoyant, like all unhappy women. One wrong note would upset the whole edifice.

"Where are you taking me?" she asked in a timid voice. She was like the big bad wolf, trying to trick little Red Riding Hood into her confidence before gobbling her up.

"Chérie," I said again, and my voice faltered. "I'm afraid to take you to a restaurant where you might be seen. It would be too great a risk, and unfair to you. A few weeks ago, when I felt very low and unhappy, I went to the most obscure restaurant in town, way down on La Cienega. And who should come in? Your husband and a blonde!"

I asked Joe and Eleanor's forgiveness for betraying them. It was untrue, too, which made the whole thing worse.

"My husband and that blonde . . ." she said. And the big bad wolf showed his long nose and his sharp teeth under the pretty bonnet. "Who was she?" she questioned, knowing too well whom I meant.

"I never saw her before. Some little blonde thing. I don't like young girls; that's why I didn't bother to look close."

"How long ago was that?" she asked. And her voice was as tense as a wound-up watch spring.

"Oh . . . a couple of months ago . . . I don't remember exactly!" I said casually.

"You didn't know Joe then," she said. But she couldn't catch an old hand so easily.

"That's right—I didn't know him . . . but who can forget a beard like his? I couldn't. I'm collecting beavers." I laughed. "And his is an extraordinary one! He counted three points in my game. When M-G-M gave him my telephone number and I met him, I remembered his face at once. A pointed beaver, rather ethereal: three points! Then the little blonde came into my mind. You came into the cutting room—remember—so I didn't mention to Mr. Sherman that I had seen him before in rather incriminating circumstances. My sense of decency prevented it. And that's why I don't want to take you to a restaurant, however obscure. Just the wrong person might come in! I'm taking you home to my place. It's rather primitive, but I feel safe there . . . and I'd know you would be safe."

I kept on talking until we arrived, because I was afraid she would ask more questions. But her mind was busy with my lie, and she didn't say a word even when the taxi stopped. I had been holding the fare in my left hand all the while to make a quick exit.

We entered the apartment building through the side door and I took the first elevator in order not to run the gauntlet of watchers in the hall. But Miss Bowden at the desk called me: "Mr. Bernet . . . here're some messages!"

"I'll get them later," I said and shoved Mrs. Sherman quickly into the elevator.

"Why don't you look at them?" she asked, with suppressed curiosity. She was already beginning to pry into my private life.

"I'm out with you tonight, and nothing else matters!" I said gallantly, and the elevator door opened.

When I opened the door to my room, she noticed the

table and the flowers at once. "You scoundrel," she said coquettishly. And if she'd had a fan, she'd have tapped me with it.

I helped her take off her coat. She was still dressed in that tailor-made outfit. It seemed to be her best dress, but not so new anymore. It bulged at various spots where she had put on weight in the last few years. She slumped down on my divan and crossed her tiny feet, asked for a cigarette, and smoked like a woman not used to it.

"A drink?" I asked her and opened my bottle of Pernod. I had to pour a couple of drinks into her quickly. That would make everything easier. I was as calm as an actor who has played in *Chu Chin Chow* for five years running. There was no need to think. Everything ran smoothly.

"To you, chérie," I said, and drank carefully, not to get tight. I had to keep myself under perfect control. She emptied her glass and leaned back, her eyes closed. But when I thought she had relaxed into a pleasant dream, she suddenly asked sharply: "What do you want?"

She opened her eyes, and I looked into black, cold transparent stones. She was not easy to fool.

"Dinner," I laughed lightheartedly. "To eat is the second most important thing in life!" That was a definite hint that flattered her and removed her suspicions for a few minutes.

I went into the kitchen, took the cold meat and the other things out of the icebox, and while I was busy arranging the table, she stood behind me. I didn't dare turn around. I had the feeling she was swinging an ax that would crash down on my skull any moment.

But she sat down without a word and began to eat.

I wasn't hungry at all. I took a second drink and filled her glass, too. She emptied it as if she were drinking water. I didn't offer her a third drink for fear my plan to make her drunk would be too plain. She waited, and when I didn't reach for the bottle, she helped herself to a big swig.

"Careful," I warned her. "You don't know how potent that stuff is!"

But she laughed, completely sure of my sincerity, and began to eat heartily.

"You're a nice boy, Pierre," she said. "I don't know what you're up to, but you're nice. I wish I'd met you twenty years ago."

This was my wish, too, at the moment, and I threw her a devoted glance.

"It's never too late . . . " I said hypocritically. She had to be stuffed with commonplace expressions. Her concierge's soul was easily impressed by them.

She finished eating, and we walked back into the living room. She sat down again, very happy, prepared to talk about herself.

I studied her as a scientist studies a dissected frog. She was repulsive. It was not that she was ugly, taking her feature by feature, but her soul was mirrored in her face. I believe that people can stay beautiful forever, if they will only avoid evil thoughts. But she had nothing but unkind thoughts, and enjoyed them. I feel sorry only for people who are struggling and getting nowhere. But this woman was the personification of evil. Everything she did showed her evil mind and irritated me. Even her small mannerisms, her Balkan accent, the way she held her cigarette in fat, pointed fingers, the way she ate and drank, cocked her head and flirted; the way her belly bulged in her tight skirt; her dimpled hands, her platinum hair . . .

But still I gazed into her eyes and played the devoted lover.

"Did I tell you that I wanted a divorce from Joe?— But now I'm going to withdraw it." She began talking about her dearest subject.

"Please . . . don't mention things like that to me . . . it only hurts me," I said, and she smiled, convinced of her power over me.

"Last night I saw that little prostitute he's in love with. And I gave her hell," she mused, recalling her hour of triumph.

"Please, chérie, don't talk like that," I said. And she took my distress as a compliment. "See . . . I'm a lost soul. I don't belong here. I belong across the sea, as you do. Now I have found you . . . a human being who understands my language, who thinks as I do. Please don't talk about Joe or a girl or a divorce to me . . . you're hurting me!"

As this was the truth, she was impressed and cast her eyes on me with obvious interest. The idea dawned on her that I might want more from her than a quick dinner and a brief flirtation. This idea began to fill her mind as a rising tide covers a barren shore. It was a business deal, and she thought it over shrewdly, as a horse trader considers a new buy. It was a proposition that needed careful consideration.

I gave her another drink and filled my own glass, too. My hand trembled. I was excited. I didn't want to go ahead too fast, but I could hardly wait. She was not at all intelligent. She had cunning and slyness and a certain feminine instinct. The rest was bovine acquiescence. She couldn't escape!

"What do you want, Pierre . . . don't beat around the bush. Just tell me! You must put the cards on the table."

The drinks were taking effect on her, while I became clearer-headed every minute. I felt my body sweat. The effort to stay calm nearly killed me.

"Chérie . . . I'm not eighteen any more, and you're not either. We're grown-up people . . .. we can look things square in the face and call them by their right names. Why do you waste your time and youth on things which have no future, which leave you empty and disgusted after you get through? That is wrong, chérie . . ."

Immediately she became alert and distrustful. She divined that I wanted to talk her out of her marriage with Joe and her revenge on him and the girl. Maybe she was afraid Joe had sent me.

"I know what you're thinking," I smiled sadly and took the bull by the horns. The best way to win was to turn her own argument against her.

"To make a clean sweep of it, chérie . . . I'll tell you everything. And I hope you can stand it. My interest in you is only secondary. I'm mainly interested in myself. That puts everything on an honest basis. I like you very much . . . but this is not of major importance between mature people. I want to escape the mess I've made of my life. And you're the woman to help me. If I'm too frank—please stop me. I don't want to hurt you. But I can only tell the truth. I want to feel at home again, and you can give me that feeling. I want to work again. And anybody can get work if he wants it badly enough. I want to have responsibilities, and I want to have someone with me who shares them and watches over me, advises me, and helps me to carry on. I thought of you, chérie . . . Last night I was dreaming of that little place . . ."

"Last night . . ." she said, and sat up straight. "We made our date only today, didn't we?"

I was a fool . . .

I laughed. "Chérie," I said, and placed my hand on her fat thigh. "Do you think an idea like that is born in a minute? I had the idea when I first saw you, when you came into the cutting room. You changed your dress before I left. Now—don't tell me you would have done that if you didn't like me a little . . ."

I felt sick about myself. Maybe I should end the whole affair now! How long could I stand it without giving myself away? And how could I escape her eyes, distrustful still but already thoughtful. I stepped over to the desk and took out my bankbook.

"A little over four thousand dollars," I said. "If we are careful, it should be enough."

"Show it to me," she demanded. And I gave her the book reluctantly. She studied the sum, turned back the pages and read my former meager deposits.

"I've made a pile the past few days . . . I went to the Club Femina and gambled."

She wouldn't believe that! Nobody could believe it. It was too ridiculous. Marjorie Dean might have won a hundred thousand, but I could not have brought home four. I knew that everything hung in the balance. Then I remembered the chip. I took it out of the drawer and threw it in her lap.

"Here's my initial capital," I said. "I haven't even cashed it. It brought me luck. I thought I should talk to you first. That's why I came to your office. I had no business with Mr. Sherman. I wanted to see you, to talk to you. Because I might go out again tonight and lose all of it. That's why I came to ask you first . . . "

She turned the chip. It was genuine. There must be truth in my words; the chip was evidence. She couldn't figure it out, couldn't put her finger on the flaw, so she caressed the chip and was convinced.

"All right," she said, forcing herself to believe. "I'll consider it."

I felt a tremendous rage flood my brain; it nearly drowned my self-control.

"No!" I said. "I won't wait! I can't wait! I want to leave now . . . at once . . . As soon as the banks open I'll get the money and run away. Decide . . . now! I don't want to take chances anymore. I'm sick of it, understand?"

My genuine excitement made a great impression on her. She looked at me with drunken eyes and a wide smile parted her lips.

"For once in my life I'd like to see . . ." she began, but I interrupted her. I had my hands close to her throat— it would have been so easy to lock my fingers for just a minute.

"Pierre . . . " She stood up, dazed. I filled her glass again and watched her.

"Chérie," I said, "I'll give you the money. You can take care of it. Because I'm irresponsible . . ."

"I know," she said, and pressed the little book against her breasts while she walked back and forth.

"But I insist that you cut your connections with your old life. You must write to Joe now and tell him you're quitting . . . I don't want to have another man around . . . do you hear? I must be sure of you before I can believe you. You might change your mind over night and where would I be? . . . Come on . . . do it . . . now!"

She stopped in the middle of the room. She divined

that something was wrong, that she was trapped, but she was too drunk to react to it.

"Why should I do it?" she asked, as if she were taking a last stand, listening to a last instinct of common sense.

I picked up a piece of notepaper and a pen. Then I took her by the arm and pushed her into a chair, put the pen into her hand and held her by the shoulders, my fingers at her throat.

"Write!"

I could feel her big Adam's apple move under my fingers. She couldn't fight anymore, but I, too, was almost at the end of my resistance.

"'Joe' . . . write that word . . . 'Joe. You can have the divorce if you give me a hundred dollars a month. I'll tell you where I am in due course. And you can send the papers to me. I'll sign them provided the alimony is paid and all my belongings delivered to me.'"

She wrote. The mercenary clause in it broke her last resistance. She had no will of her own. I had won!

"Sign!" I said, and watched her write her name under the letter. Her first name was Anita!

Immediately, I snatched the letter from her hands and put it into an envelope, wrote the address on the cover. I had done it too quickly. My haste was too obvious . . . for she looked at me with new suspicion.

But I didn't care any longer! I put a stamp on it and walked to the door.

"Where're you going?" she asked. She tried to pull herself together. But I left and ran downstairs. The letter had to be mailed at once.

18

Halfway downstairs, I realized I was drunk. I had made a mistake, had shown too clearly how interested I was in that letter. She could easily walk out on me now and go home, catch the letter when it arrived, and all my effort would have been wasted.

But she didn't have her brain under control. She still wasn't sure of my motives, and would hesitate to leave, at least until I had returned with some explanation.

When I got to the landing that overlooked the big hall, I saw two men talking to Miss Bowden. One had cauliflower ears, the other reddish hair and glasses. Marshall's mercuries! I wondered where he hid them when he didn't need them. In the back room of a shabby hotel, where, hats on head, they played cards until the boss telephoned them to come out? Didn't they have anything to do but play gangster all day long? They might have names like Jack the Blood and Flat-ear Harry.

I walked over to the desk and they didn't see me come until I butted into their conversation with a polite, "Pardon me, gentlemen!"

They froze. I grinned into their faces. They wouldn't dare shoot now. They hunted in pairs, were only brave when shooting in the back, when jumping into cars with phony license plates and driving away before you could say Jake Rabinowitz.

Ito, the Filipino boy, came along just then to collect the last mail on his way home. Ito was very reliable; it was safer to give him the letter than to mail it myself. They wouldn't stop him.

"Hello, Ito," I said. "Here's a letter. Be sure and mail it, won't you?"

"Very sure, sir," Ito grinned. "Never lost a letter in eighteen years." And he walked out with a friendly good night.

I saw my two gangster friends look after him uneasily. They were on a spot. Should they run after Ito and get the envelope, which might contain nothing of importance, or should they stay here and play innocent?

They decided to stay.

"Anything for me, Miss Bowden?" I seemed not to recognize the men who had beaten me up. And they didn't know what to do. They had one-track minds, and I was moving on a different track.

"These gentlemen were asking for you," said Miss Bowden in her friendly way. "And here're some messages . . ."

"Just a minute, please!" I smiled at the men and read the slips. "Oh . . . from Miss Dean . . . all three of them. She can be a nuisance, can't she! I wish she'd leave me alone!"

Miss Bowden's eyes grew round with surprise. The men got their second shock. Suddenly they turned and walked out. It was getting too hot for them. They didn't want to be drawn into an embarrassing conversation.

Miss Bowden looked after them dumfounded.

"What did they want?" I asked, rereading the messages to give her time to recover.

"They were inquiring about you," Miss Bowden said, still astonished. "I asked them if they wanted me to phone up. But they said no, they'd just wait for you.

Funny . . . and what manners!"

"They haven't any! But they'll wait for me, don't worry! I thought they'd bring me my hat!" I said mysteriously and left her in a state of wonder and concern.

I was sure they wouldn't catch Ito now. He has a small car and I had heard him drive off. He was miles away already.

I took the elevator up to my floor, tiptoed to my room and opened the door quickly.

Anita stood at my desk. She had pulled out all the drawers and dug through them. She seemed to have sobered up considerably, and nothing of the gentle demeanor she had assumed before remained. She turned, ready to fight if I were Joe. She held Eleanor's picture in her hand.

I locked the door behind me, cold and intent. Here was the moment toward which, unconsciously, I had steered, never swerving from my course. Here it was, the fate I had waited and wished for. There was no retreat now. It was the summing up of my life.

"Where did you get this picture?" she asked, choking with fury and hatred. She knew that she had been deceived.

"Looking through my drawers already?" I asked, and stepped closer. There was something inflexible in my voice that made her still more furious.

"You know her . . ." she said.

I took the picture from her fat hand and looked at it.

"Of course . . . it's Eleanor Marr," I said quietly. "She tried to kill herself last night. She didn't succeed . . . You didn't succeed," I said, and was careful to stand between her and the door.

She sat down. Her eyes had changed color. They were dull with hatred. She was searching desperately for the word that would hurt me most.

"I've known Eleanor for a long time. I'm in love with her," I continued calmly. I took the chair opposite her, but was still ready to jump.

"Then everything you told me was a lie."

"Of course. I even forged the bank deposits. I have no money. All I have is eighteen dollars and fifty cents."

"You just wanted me to sign that letter . . . to help her . . ." she said.

"Exactly," I said. "You've got it right . . . but I wanted to help Joe, too. He's my friend."

She looked at me in silence. She didn't know what was at the bottom of my mind. She still didn't know she was licked.

"So you're in love with her," she said. "Well, if you're a man, why don't you fight for her . . . why do you give her to Joe?"

"That's something you wouldn't understand," I said. "She's not in love with me. And that settles it!"

There was a pause. She got up. And I rose, too.

"I don't know what you're after," she said, "but the whole scheme is ridiculous!"

"Not so ridiculous as you think!" I said. I felt the muscles of my arms tightening, as if I had a cramp. I moved my fingers to relieve the tension.

"Well"—she took her hat, shrugged her shoulders—"it's childish . . . I can deny the letter any time. I see your plan. You lured me up here, and maybe you'll swear that you seduced me, to make me guilty. No! . . . Not a chance! I'm going from here to a doctor and have him certify that nothing of the sort has happened."

"You don't have to do that," I said. I was tired and disgusted with all this talking that dragged on endlessly. I wanted to silence her voice and get her out of my sight; I hated her so much that her presence was an unbearable torture. I looked into her eyes and they mirrored my mood. I must have frightened her out of her wits. She stood motionless, stared at me. Her lower lip trembled and she broke into tears.

"No . . ." she said in a squeaky voice.

Her sudden helplessness made it easy for me. I wanted to crush her, her face, her body; she stood in my way; without her there would be a clear road to the end. I had to get rid of her, dispose of her. There was only one thing to do. She mustn't talk anymore, or think, or walk about. She had to disappear. She had to be destroyed . . .

My hands ached when I tried to open them. I had been trying to open them for a minute or more, but my fingers were locked with cramp. They closed tighter and tighter the more I tried to loosen them. The blood stopped in my wrists; it hurt; I wanted to be rid of this unbearable pain; I wanted to cry out, but no sound came from my lips. My teeth hurt, too. I had bitten my tongue, and blood filled my mouth slowly until I swallowed.

My hands finally loosened. Her body slumped to the floor. I heard my breathing in the room, like that of someone else. I looked at my hands. They were swollen. I wanted to cool them, to wash them at once, with green soap and hot water. I wanted to change my shirt, my suit, my socks and shoes. I wanted nothing to remind me of this moment.

Her bulging body lay stretched out on the floor. It

was the second dead face I had seen in my life. Niven first . . . now she. I was sorry for Niven. He had tried, right to the end.

But she hadn't. Her face still repelled me. It was ugly, bad, inhuman. She couldn't harm anyone anymore.

I went to the sink, washed, and came back.

She was still lying in the same position. I took her by the arms and pulled her into the bathroom. It was like dragging a trunk. I lifted her—how heavy she was, her big legs dangling, her small shoes waving helplessly. She slid into the tub, and I turned the water on. It splashed over her dress, soaked her, and covered her slowly.

I had killed her and now the water began to drown her. I watched her face until the water had reached it. And there it was—the water flowed over her face and changed her features. The mouth became soft, curled into a smile, a holy smile, a smile of happiness, of abandon and content.

I left the water running slowly to keep her clean; it ran out through the drain. Before I went out I crossed myself. I hadn't made that gesture since I was a child . . . twenty years ago. Now it came back to me quite naturally.

I switched off the lights in the bathroom and closed the door. I listened. I couldn't hear the water running. That consoled me. Her grave was silent.

I went back into my room and stretched out on the couch. I fell asleep at once. It was as if a hand had switched off my thinking with soft fingers. I felt it getting dark, but, like a bright light suddenly extinguished, the last few moments left their image on my retina.

19

I haven't left my room for two days. To be precise, for two days and three nights. I've asked the switchboard not to ring me because I am working hard. I didn't want to receive any outside calls, any mail. I didn't even want to have my room cleaned.

My private phone has a secret number, as is customary in this town full of secrets. People feel more important if their names are not in the directory. The very snobbish ones even change their private numbers from time to time, to give the new one to their friends as a gesture of intimacy.

Only a few people know my private number. Eleanor is one of them. I am waiting for her call. She will phone as soon as the letter arrives.

In the meantime, I'm writing these pages.

I am writing them to tell how it happened that the only decent act of my life was murdering that thing in my bathroom. To prove that a murder can be a merciful operation: the cutting of a cancer out of other people's lives.

I write also to make clear to myself what I have done. And to make myself aware of my own happiness.

I write, too, to help Eleanor and Joe to be happy. They mustn't think badly of me. I'm sure they won't when they read this.

And I must write because I am waiting for Eleanor's call.

I haven't eaten for several days. The first day it was unpleasant. I felt like a baby who has had his bottle taken away. The second day it didn't matter anymore.

This third night, I am beginning to float. My mind is as clear as a flawless crystal. And I am happy about this, too.

When I step to the window and look out, I can see Marshall's men waiting for me. They do it quite cleverly. Sometimes a car waits there. Sometimes two men just stand there for half an hour, talking. Sometimes another car waits. And sometimes there is no one to be seen at all. They arouse no suspicion, but I am sure they're guarding the house like a treasure. They have found out my private number, and from time to time they check up to be sure I haven't climbed over the roof and run away. I am glad to answer the phone. I want to assure them that I'm still in my room.

I'm sure I'm not stupid. I am as intelligent as other people. Only my mind has always seen the world out of focus and projected a distorted picture on my brain. I have finally straightened that out.

I know that nobody can exist without some ideal to live for. Joe had his religion; Anita, her hatred; Eleanor, her love. Marshall—Marjorie—Jerry . . . Even Niven had something to live for and to die for. They may have been right or wrong, but they were not empty, completely selfish, as I was.

If you spit at life, life spits back at you. If you settle in a new country, you must throw your past away and begin over again, like being reborn. You must adjust your heart and your conscience, your emotions, your love. But if you're too conceited, too arrogant to make any possible concession, you're doomed to fail. And you'll be buried with your ill will and your failure.

My unrest has gone. My fire is almost burned out; it smolders only for the few hours I still have to live.

I've done my share, at the very last moment.

I have to do a little summing up.

When did I read Shakespeare last? When did I open the Bible for the last time. When did I look at a picture by Rembrandt, by Van Gogh? When did I listen to Beethoven's *Seventh* or Handel's *Messiah* for the last time? And when I listened and looked, did it ever occur to me that it might be for the last time in my life?

Jerry left me without saying good night; he left me in the lavatory at the Femina. Joe—he seemed to know; he looked into my eyes. Little Emily—of her no impression remains, I don't know where I lost her. Eleanor gave me a smile on my way.

That's it. People don't leave you with a curtain speech, like in a play. They enter your life with some irrelevant remark, and walk out with an unfinished sentence.

The telephone rings.

Marshall's men are checking up. They're beginning to be impatient. But I know they'll wait. They have to wait. Marshall will do anything to keep me from talking.

The telephone rings again.

Eleanor!

"Hello, Pierre," she says. I can tell that she is breathless with excitement.

"Oh, hello, Eleanor . . . what's new . . . how do you feel?"

"All right . . . but a letter came," she says. She can't keep it to herself a second longer. She is bursting with the news.

"A letter . . . what letter?" I ask.

"Mrs. Sherman has left . . . for good . . . she's setting

Joe free . . . he's got it in writing . . . her writing!"

"You don't say," I answer. And I am really excited for her. "You see, you should never give up hope. There's a deep instinct for decency in every human being! I'm so glad, Eleanor!"

"I only hope she sticks to her promise . . . she might change her mind," Eleanor says, and, as always, she wants to have my assurance. She believes in me. Trusts my judgment.

"She won't say another word," I promise. And the unconscious irony of my words does not strike me.

"Pierre . . . I'm so glad . . ." she says. And I see her smiling. "I hope to see you soon."

"Yes," I answer.

I hold the receiver as if I were embracing her, as if she were standing here beside me and I held her soft, young shoulders in my arms. I close my eyes and listen to her voice.

"*Au revoir*, Pierre," she says.

"Good-bye, Eleanor," I say. "I'm sure you will be very happy."

The phone clicks.

There's nothing more to say.

I'm going to put on my hat and coat, and I'll walk downstairs, Eleanor's picture in my pocket.

The deep-sea fish will burst. His soul will be bared. But before he dies, he will have seen the light.

THE END

Dana Wilson was a wife, mother, actress, and author. Born Dorothy Natoli (later shortened to Natol) in New York City on January 3, 1922, she took the name Dana when she moved to Los Angeles to pursue her acting career, and became Dana Wilson when she married the original Batman actor, Lewis Wilson, in 1941.

Alongside her short acting career, Dana wrote two novels—*Make With The Brains Pierre* (1946), also released under the titles *Scenario for Murder* and *Uneasy Virtue*—and *Florinda* (1977). *Florinda* was produced as a West End stage musical *La Cava* in 2000, with Dana writing the book for the show.

Dana Wilson is perhaps best known as Dana Broccoli, after her second marriage to film producer Albert R "Cubby" Broccoli in 1959. Cubby Broccoli went on to create and produce the James Bond film series, and although she is never credited on the Bond films themselves, Dana is acknowledged as a powerful force in shaping the longest running cinema franchise in history. She is also the mother of the current Bont Bond producers Michael G Wilson and Barbara Broccoli.

Dana Broccoli passed away in Beverly Hills on February 29, 2004.

www.ingramcontent.com/pod-product-compliance
Lightning Source LLC
Chambersburg PA
CBHW072359170726
48002CB00018B/336